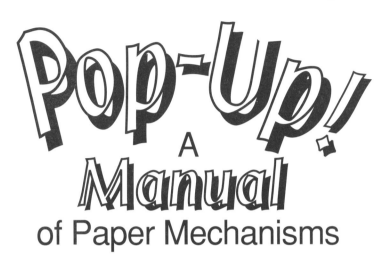

A Manual

of Paper Mechanisms

Duncan Birmingham

Tarquin Publications

For Jess

If you have enjoyed this book then there may be other Tarquin books which would interest you, including 'Paper Engineering' and 'Up-pops' by Mark Hiner and several other titles by Duncan Birmingham.

They are available from Bookshops, Toyshops, Art/Craft shops or, in case of difficulty directly from Tarquin Publications. For an up-to-date catalogue, please write to the publishers at the address below. Alternatively, see us on the Internet at http://www.tarquin-books.demon.co.uk

© 2000: Duncan Birmingham
© 1997: First Edition
I.S.B.N.: 1 899618 09 0
Cover: Paul Chilvers
Printing: Five Castles Press, Ipswich   All rights reserved

Tarquin Publications
Stradbroke
Diss
Norfolk IP21 5JP
England

This manual offers a working guide to the intriguing mechanisms that leap up from pop-up books or cards. The only realistic way to understand the potential of pop-up technology and to learn how such mechanisms are designed and constructed is to make a wide range of them yourself. Appreciating how the standard mechanisms work and why they sometimes fail is an essential step towards creating original designs of your own.

True pop-ups are based on only three simple ideas. They are known as the 'V-Fold', the 'Parallelogram' and the '45° Fold'. It is the development of these three ideas which creates the wealth and richness which this field of artistic activity has to offer. A particular feature of this collection is how the mechanisms can be grouped into families and how one idea can grow out of another. The manual starts by introducing some simple and elementary designs and then shows how they can be extended, modified and combined to produce sophisticated fold-away paper sculptures, with the potential to illustrate a wide range of stories, topics and notions.

Although the title of this manual is 'Pop-up', it also deals with the slides, pull strips and rotating disks which commonly are found in the imaginative children's books, loosely referred to as 'Pop-up Books'. Since they are made of paper, the general name is 'paper engineering'. Use this manual as a compendium of paper engineering ideas and flick through the pages until you see a design to make. Alternatively, work systematically through it and so acquire a comprehensive understanding of the whole subject.

On pages 4 and 5 there is a list of the mechanisms which shows how they relate to each other. Each mechanism has a reference number and they are grouped under subheadings showing how a particular idea can be developed. Making the first mechanism in each family group will give a good basic understanding of what that particular pop-up technique can offer. The more distant relatives of some of the mechanisms are also listed. These will be useful to advanced paper engineers with a particular design problem to solve or to students seeking a fuller understanding of the possibilities of pop-up and other paper engineering designs.

Before you start to make up designs of your own, read pages 6 to 8. They cover the materials you need, the basic vocabulary and symbols used in the book and also the best order in which to work. Once you have started, it will not be long before something fails to work as you expected or hoped. Page 9 offers suggestions about problem solving and trouble shooting. After pointing out the most common causes of potential difficulties there is advice on how important it is to start by making quick roughs of a new idea.

The creative potential in paper engineering is very great and hopefully this manual will set you off on a rewarding trail which will give many hours of interest and pleasure.

LIST OF MECHANISMS

To explore a particular mechanism and see how it can be adapted, consider the other mechanisms in the same subgroup. Where other mechanisms are mentioned, further ideas and developments are to be found there.

SIMPLE V-FOLDS

MODIFIED V-FOLDS

MULTIPLE V-FOLDS

ASYMMETRICAL V-FOLDS

THE PARALLELOGRAM

COMBINING PARALLELOGRAMS AND V-FOLDS

TWO PARALLEL STICKING STRIPS

JUTTING EXTENSIONS

MATERIALS

Paper or Card?
Cartridge paper can be used but it should not be lighter than 135 gsm. The ideal weight is 220 gsm. This is the type of card which is used for postcards.

Scissors or Craft-knife?
A pair of scissors is adequate for cutting out most of the pop-up mechanisms. However for the pull-strip designs a craft-knife is essential. A sharp edge is vital so the type of craft-knife with extending 'snap-off' blades is ideal.

Scoring
Scoring is very important. Using a ball-point pen which has run out of ink creates a strong fold, as the paper's fibres are compressed rather than cut.

Glue
A clear, solvent-based adhesive is best. The new 'Gel' types are probably the most effective as they can be more easily controlled. Water based glues dry too slowly and may wrinkle the card and the stick-glues, which are sold for paper craft, are not really strong or permanent enough for this type of work.

Pencil & Ruler
A propelling 'clutch' pencil or a hard ordinary pencil is advised.
A ruler is essential for scoring long straight creases. A steel ruler is strongly recomended for cutting against when using a craft-knife.

Cutting-board
This is really necessary to save your surfaces. Thick cardboard, like the back of a drawing pad, will do, but a commercial mat is best of all.

Paper-knife
When sticking pieces into place, a paper knife is very useful for pressing down corners and edges that are hard to reach.

Drawing Instruments
Many lengths and angles have to be measured and drawn very accurately, so a set square, a protractor and a pair of compasses will be needed.

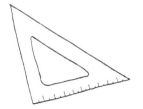  

BASICS

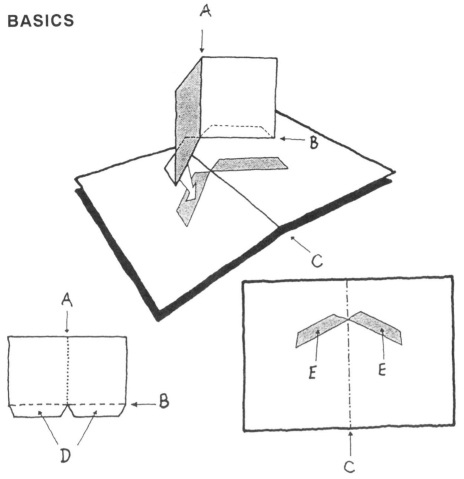

Throughout this manual the double-page to which the pop-up is glued is referred to as the **Base**.

There are three kinds of folded line:

1. Valley folds, marked A in the diagrams above.
The crease goes back, away from the viewer.

2. Mountain folds, marked B in the diagrams above.
The crease comes forward, towards the viewer.

3. The Spine, marked C in the diagrams above.
The fold down the centre of the base.

There are also:

1. Gluing-tabs, marked D in the diagrams above.
They are the little flaps that the glue is spread on when sticking a piece onto the base or another pop-up piece. These are usually about 1cm. wide. Any narrower and they tend to pull off.

2. Sticking-strips, marked E in the diagrams above.
They are the areas on the base or other pieces that the gluing-tabs glue to.

WORKING ORDER

1. Measure and draw out the design.
Accuracy when measuring lengths and angles is very important to create mechanisms which move and fold away cleanly.

2. Score all the fold lines.
Scoring makes for a much sharper and more accurate fold. It is easiest to do this before the individual pieces are cut out.

3. Cut out the pop-up pieces.

4. Having scored and cut out the pop-up piece, fold it along each crease and firmly run your finger nail along each fold. Then fold it back on itself and do the same thing again. The more thoroughly creased and easily folding the better. The fold is the hinge of the mechanism. Creasing it well is like oiling a hinge.

5. Think before you glue. Sometimes flaps become inaccessible as the construction builds up. Where this may be a difficulty the gluing order is explained.

6. When a mechanism uses several pieces, it is best to close the base and press it firmly after each new piece is glued on. If you leave it until the mechanism is complete, it may develop unwanted creases.

It is normal to glue all the gluing tabs on each pop-up piece to the base before the base is folded shut. However there is another method which is very effective.

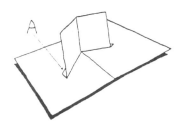 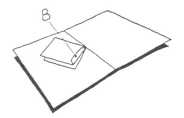 

1. Put glue on one flap and stick it to the base.	2. Fold the pop-up piece into its closed position, then put glue on the other flap.	3. Close the base. The second flap then finds its natural sticking position.

PROBLEM SOLVING

Occasionally a mechanism doesn't work properly and this is usually due to inaccuracy somewhere. If you do have any difficulties, the most common problems can be tracked down by checking this list.

If the mechanism 'lists' when the page is open, or crumples as the page is closed:
1. Check that the lengths and angles have the measurements which were intended.
2. Check that the lines that should be parallel are parallel.

If the mechanism moves stiffly, or tends to 'hang' in the closed position:
1. It may not have been scored and creased sufficiently.
2. The glue may have oozed and gummed up the works.
3. The card is too thin and is bending where it shouldn't.
4. The card is too thick and isn't bending where it should.

If the pull-strip moves stiffly when pulled:
1. The strip may be being gripped by the page. Check that the slots and sleeves are wide enough and that slits are long enough.
2. If the sleeves are too loose the pull-strip can wobble diagonally. This will cause it to stick.
3. Check for excess glue that's oozed.

DESIGN HINTS

1. When working out a new design always make a rough version first. This is advisable in order to check that pieces fit together and fold away as planned. Having a working model in front of you also makes it far easier to visualise extending and modifying the design.

2. Colouring and decorating the design is easiest while the pieces are still flat and before it is glued into place.

3. When making up new designs, consider the effect of cutting 'windows' in the pop-up planes. Experiment by cutting away parts and to see how little card is actually needed. In this way you can develop exciting pop-up shapes.

4. Remember that the actual mechanism may often only be the 'muscle' which lifts larger images which are stuck on later.

5. Gluing-tabs are normally positioned so that they fold back and are hidden from view by the pop-up piece. However they may fold forward and become a part of the visual design. For extra strength they can also be inserted through a slit and glued to the underside of the card.

1. THE SIMPLE V-FOLD

This is one of the most simple pop-up mechanisms, and one of the most useful. In this, its most basic form, it can be enhanced by cutting the pop-up planes into exciting shapes.

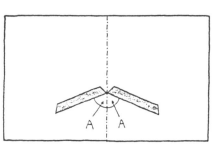

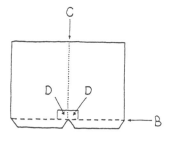

On the base:
Angles A must be the same.
They must be less than 90°.
Try making them about 70°.

On the pop-up piece:
The scored line B is straight.
The central crease C is vertical
Angles D are both 90°.

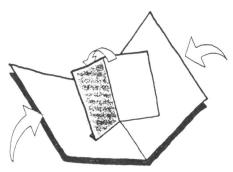

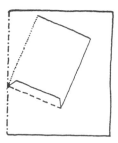

As the base closes the pop-up piece folds down backwards (away from the viewer). Before gluing check where the pop-up piece will fold away to. If it is tall it must be positioned near the front of the base to prevent it jutting out when the base is closed.

2. MULTIPLE SIMPLE POP-UP PIECES

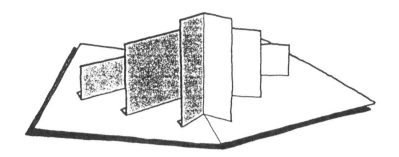

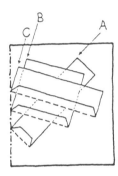

Closed position

With several pieces popping-up from the base, the danger is that as the base closes and the pieces fold down their central creases (A,B,C) will clash.

To avoid this the central crease of a piece should either fold back less than the one behind it (crease A folds back less than B); or they should fold down parallel to each other (crease B is parallel to C).

The smaller the angles between the sticking-strips and the spine, the less the piece will lean back as the base closes.

Because angles D are less than angles E, crease A leans back less than crease B. Because angles E and F are the same, sticking-strips G and H are parallel, this makes central creases B lie parallel to C when the base is closed.

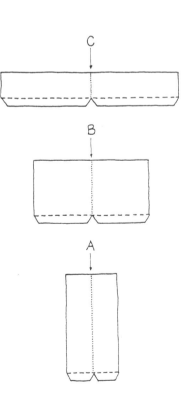

3. THE V-FOLD POINTING FORWARDS

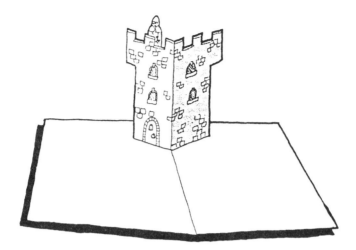

As the base closes the pop-up piece folds down towards the viewer. Therefore tall pop-up pieces need to be positioned near the back, or top, of the base. This is useful as it leaves more foreground clear for illustrations or text.

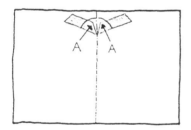

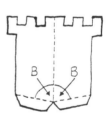

On the base: Angles A must match each other. Try: A = 70°.
On the pop-up piece: Angles B must match each other. Try: B = 80°.
Angles A must always be smaller than angles B or the base can't open out flat.

When the V-Fold points forward, if angles C are 90° the pop-up piece will tend to sag forwards unless the base is opened out perfectly flat. Making angles C less than 90° cures the sag effect. In Mechanism **1** the pop-up piece folds away backwards so the sag is away from the viewer and actually enhances the visual effect.

4. VARYING THE V-FOLD ANGLES

The angle at which the pop-up rises from the base, and the sharpness of its central crease, can be varied by adjusting the angles A and B. Angles A must always be bigger than angles B. Angles B must be less than 90°.

 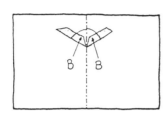 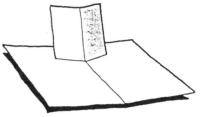

With angles A less than 90° the pop-up piece will always lean back.
Try: A = 75°, B = 55°.

 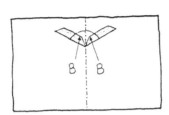 

If A gets more acute, and B stays the same : the pop up will lean back more.
Try: A = 65°, B = 55°.

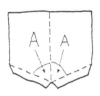 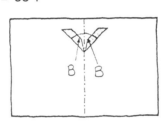 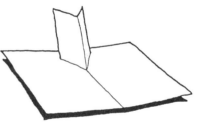

If A remains the same, but B is made more acute : the pop up piece will stand more upright and its central crease will become sharper.
Try: A = 65°, B = 45°.

 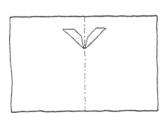 

Angles A can be obtuse, then the pop-up will lift but remain leaning forward.
Try: A = 100°, B = 45°.

When designing your own pop-ups, the best way to find the shape you want is by experiment. Also, try rotating the base, either viewing it from the other end, or alternatively using the base vertically rather than horizontally.

To make asymmetrical variations, see Mechanism **31**.

5. THE V-FOLD WITH ADDED CUTS & CREASES

The simple V-Fold can be changed into a range of different pop-up shapes by simply adding two symmetrical creases and a cut.

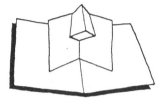
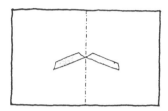

The base in all these variations is the same:
Two sticking-strips symmetrically placed either side of the spine.

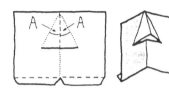

Angles A are the same.

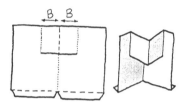

Lengths B are the same, the additional folds are parallel to the central fold.

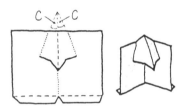

Angles C are the same.

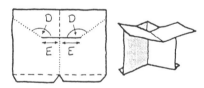

Angles D are the same, lengths E are the same.

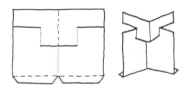

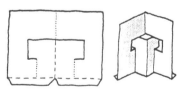

The modifications should be done before the pop-up is stuck to the base. Make sure that the additional fold lines are very well creased.

This mechanism is worth experimenting with, interesting pop-up shapes can often be "found" rather than planned.

6. V-FOLD WITH PROJECTIONS

Asymmetrical jutting-out pieces can be created by making cuts that start and finish on the pop-up's central crease line. The central fold of the pop-up is not scored or creased between the ends of the cut line.

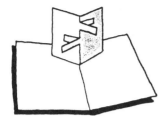 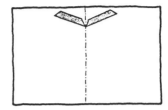

The base for all these examples is the same:
Two sticking-strips symmetrically placed either side of the spine.

To construct the pop-up piece:
1. Draw the central crease.
2. Make the additional cut.
   Ensure that it starts and finishes on the line of the central crease.
3. Score the central fold line.
   Make sure that this crease only meets the cut and doesn't cross it.
4. For the angles on the bottom of the pop-up piece, refer to Mechanism **4**.
5. Using the tabs on the bottom edge, stick the pop-up to the base.

This type of pop-up can be extended by gluing extra pieces onto the jutting out planes.

7. BEAKS, NOSES, MOUTHS

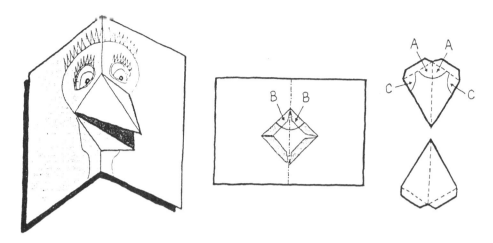

The beak is made of two pop-up pieces, as the base closes one folds away up, the other down.

The beak's shape can be adjusted by changing the pairs of angles - A, B, & C.
Angles A must be larger than angles B or the base won't open fully.
Try angles: A = 60°, B = 30°, C = 90°.

As the base opens, the amount that the beak's tip moves is determined by angles B.

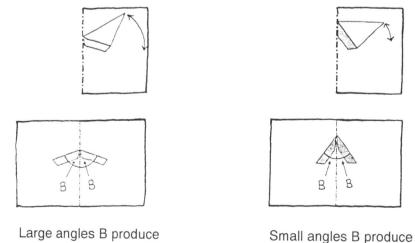

Large angles B produce
a large movement.

Small angles B produce
a smaller movement.

8. VARYING BEAK SHAPES

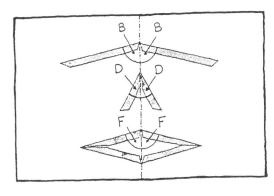

THE CAP:
The bottom edge of the pop-up piece is straight.
Angle A is bigger than angle B.
When the base is open the front of the peak will point slightly up.
Try: A = 60°, B = 50°.

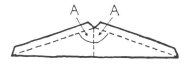

THE NOSE:
The bottom edge is cut to a point.
Angle C is bigger than angle D.
With the base open the tip of the nose will point down.
Try: C = 40°, D = 20°.

THE MOUTH:
The bottom edge is straight.
Angles E are the same as angles F.
When the base opens the mouth closes.
Try: E = 70°, F = 70°.

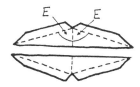

All these shapes are useful either way up. The example below shows how a "nose" can be turned upside down and adapted. Try: G = 50°, H = 30°.

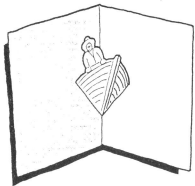

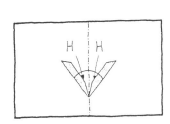

9. JAWS

As the base opens and closes this mechanism gives a great chomping effect.

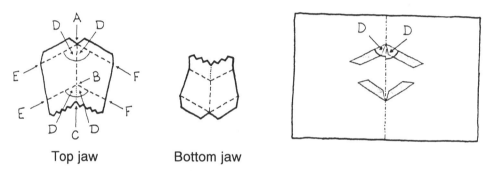

Top jaw   Bottom jaw

The key to this mechanism is the central crease on the pop-up piece.
Between points A and B is a mountain fold, Between B and C is a valley fold.

In its most simple form -
Angles marked D are all the same, both on the base, and on the pop-up piece.
The two fold lines marked E are parallel, as are the folds marked F.

The bigger angle D, the more the jaws will move as the base opens.
Try: Angle D = 70°.

Design consideration:
Normally the base will be held open at an angle with the jaws jutting forward.
Problems may occur if the base is opened out flat, this will make the pop-up
pieces flatten out too and cause the two jaws to clash.
There are three solutions:
1. Only use a top jaw.
2. Move the sticking-strips for the jaws further apart and/or shorten
lengths AB and BC,
3. Adjust the angles using the information opposite.

10. VARYING JAW ANGLES

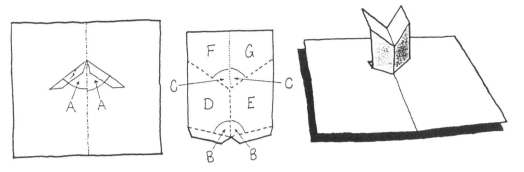

Varying the pairs of angles A, B, and C changes the shape of the Jaw. A is always smaller than B. If angle B is bigger than C the central crease of the gully hangs roughly parallel to the spine. Try - A = 60°, B = 80°, C = 45°.

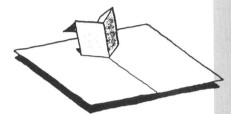

If angle B is the same as angle C:-
Planes F & G will form a gully
sloping back towards the base.
Try - A = 60°, B = 80°, C = 80°.

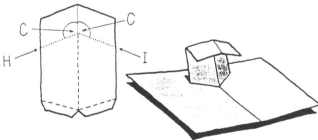

11. If angle C is more than 90°
lines H and I become valley folds,
then planes F and G fold forwards
instead of backwards.

12.
The shapes and angles of the jaw
can also be adjusted by taking a
bite out of planes F & G. Keep it
symmetrical by making angles C
the same.
Remember to add a gluing tab, J.

After the mechanism is mounted on the base, larger images can be stuck onto
any of the four planes: D, E, F, G.

The base can be used either vertically or horizontally.
To adjust the angles between the base and planes D & E, see Mechanism **4**.
For asymmetrical variations see Mechanism **32**.

13.   SCULPTING THE V-FOLD

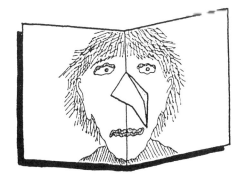

The key to these mechanisms is a "bite", or wedge, that is cut out of the pop-up piece. This enables the pop-up to bend in mysterious ways.
Here the "bite" is taken out of the end of the nose. This creates a curved bend in the planes on each side of the central crease.

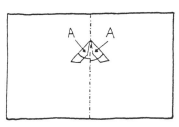
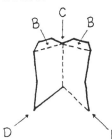

In all these designs the angles A, on the base, are always approximately 45°. Adjusting them slightly, significantly changes the pop-up shape.
Tabs B stick the pop-ups to the base.

To construct this mechanism:
Draw the two sides of the pop-up piece so that they are symmetrical around the central crease, line C. One side of the "bite" is cut, line D. The other side is scored, line E, and a tab added. The tab sticks under the opposite side of the "bite" and pulls the pop-up into shape.

14.

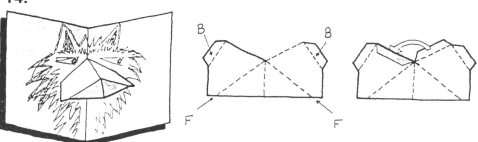

Here the "bite" is taken out of the pop-up piece between the tabs, B.
Adding creases F changes the projecting end from a curve into a more angular construction.   It's useful to compare this with Mechanism **12**.

15.

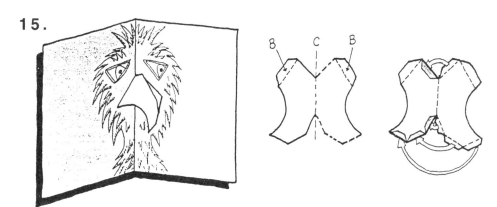

To make a big curve take a "bite" out of both ends of the central fold, C.
To draw it up: break the curve down into a series of short straight lines,
make the two sides symmetrical around line C. Finally, add tabs to one side,
these pull the curve into shape.

16.

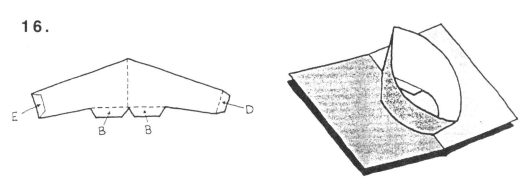

Glue the pop-up piece into a loop, D sticks to E. Then use tabs B to stick it to
the base. Finally, tailor the bottom edge of the pop-up piece so that it fits
neatly on the open base.

17.

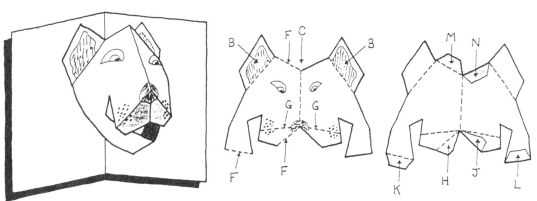

Constructing this mechanism: Make sure it's symmetrical around the centre
fold-line C. Add tabs to the three creases marked F. The two scored lines G
shape the nose. Tab H sticks under J. K sticks under L. M sticks under N.
Tabs B stick the pop-up to the base, stick these last.

18. THE V-FOLD GLUED AWAY FROM THE SPINE

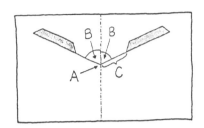

On the base: The sticking-strips stand on two lines that meet at a point on the spine, A. They both lie at the same angle to the spine B.

Length C on the base, between the sticking-strips and the spine, is the same as C on the pop-up piece, between the tabs and the central fold D.

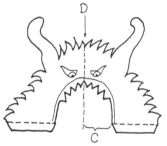

To vary the angle between the pop-up and the base, refer to Mechanisms **4** and **31**.

The pop-up piece can be made asymmetrical. The lines that the sticking-strips stand on still meet at the same point on the spine, A, and lie at the same angle to it, B.
Distance C, between the pop-up's vertical crease and the gluing-tab, is the same as C on the base. Similarly D on the pop-up piece equals D on the base.

19. BENDING SHAPES

Making the sides of the pop-up piece tall and narrow allows them to twist. Then distance A on the pop-up piece can be bigger or smaller than distance B on the base.

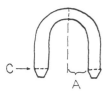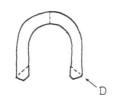

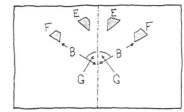

The angle of the glueing-tabs on the pop-up piece can vary, C and D. The angles on the feet must mirror each other.

The two sticking-strips on the base mirror each other: they are the same distance from the spine, B, and at the same angle to it, G.

C feet glued to areas E.

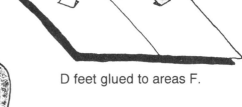

D feet glued to areas F.

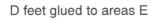

D feet glued to areas E

20.

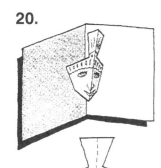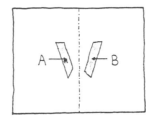

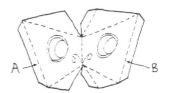

Both these designs use the same pattern of two sticking-strips placed symmetrically on each side of the spine.
The face is a cut-away version of the Nose in Mechanism **8**.
The owl's head derives from Mechanism **15**.

21. V-FOLDS ON TOP OF V-FOLDS

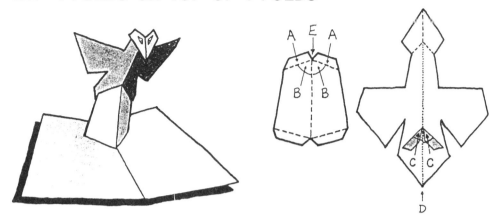

Here a V-Fold, Mechanism **3**, is used to lift other pieces above the base.
The top of the lifting-piece is pointed, it has two tabs at the top, A.
The second piece sticks onto these. Angles B are the same.
The position of the additional piece can be changed dramatically by adjusting angles B on the lifting-piece, and C on the raised piece.

To construct this mechanism: 1. Stick the lifting-piece to the page. 2. Make a central crease, D, in a second piece of card. 3. Place this card on top of the lifting piece, it can be either a mountain or a valley fold. 4. See-saw the top piece to find the best position. 5. Stick the top piece onto the two tabs. Make sure that crease D lies right up against the lifting-piece's central crease E.
6. The head of the bird on this design is made with Mechanism **11**.

Using this pointed type of lifting-piece these are the possible variations.
Before sticking any top piece on, check that the lifting-piece is tall enough to allow everything to fold away.

The effects are very different
if the first piece is placed facing
the other way on the base.

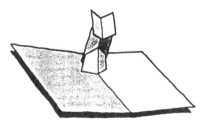

The second piece can have tabs
added to the top edge so that it
in turn lifts a third piece.

22.

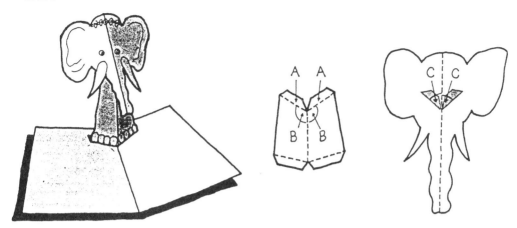

In this variation the top of the lifting-piece is made in the shape of a V.
It has two gluing-tabs, A, at the top.
Construction is the same as for Mechanism **21**, opposite.

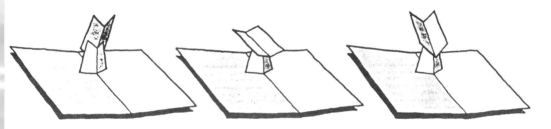

Using this type of lifting-piece these are the possible variations.

It's worth experimenting with this mechanism to grasp its full potential.

23.

With the base vertical, several pieces can be built jutting out from it. Here
the muzzle is made with Mechanism **14**.

24. COMBINING V-FOLDS

A Mechanism **3** V-Fold can lift other V-Folds stuck onto both the front and the back. Make sure that pieces stuck on the front don't hit the spine as the base closes.

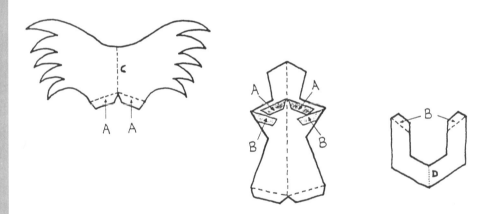

The Wings are a V-Fold stuck onto the back of the figure using tabs A.
The arms are made with a Mechanism **18** stuck onto the front using tabs B.

When making a preliminary rough, work out the angles on the additional pieces by experimentation. It is often easiest <u>not to score</u> creases C and D before sticking the extra pieces onto the body. Instead, score and fold the tabs A or B, stick the piece into place, then close the page and press it firmly so that the additional piece finds its natural folding position.
When using this method, work out one piece at a time, rather than sticking several pieces on and then closing the base on them all at once.

25. If the beak crunches against the spine as the base closes: either shorten the beak; or make the pop-up lean back more, see Mechanism **4**.

Mechanism **14** can be added to a simple V-Fold

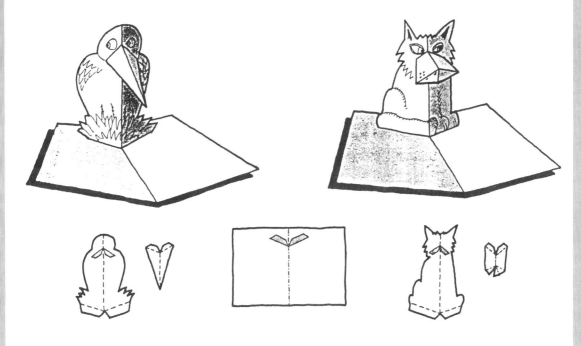

26.

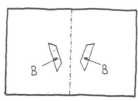

V-Folds can be added to Mechanism **20**. To construct it:
1. Stick tab A into position.
2. Stick tabs B to the base.
3. Experiment with the position of the second piece, then glue it into place using tabs C.
4. Add nose, D. Stick on E.

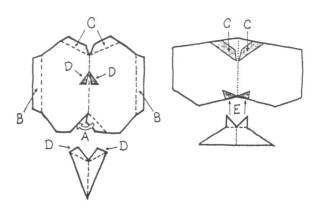

27. MULTIPLE V-FOLDS

The gullies formed between a simple V-Fold (Mechanism **3**) and the base can be used like spine folds. Small V-Fold pieces can be stuck into them. These small pieces then become the muscle for lifting larger images.

A lot of variation is possible with the small V-Fold pieces. They can be mountain folds, or valley folds, and their central creases can point towards the spine, or away from it. Angles A and B don't have to be the same.
Be careful, if angle A + B is too small the main pop-up won't be able to rise and the base cannot be fully opened.

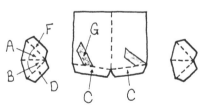

The best sticking method is as follows:-
1. Stick the V-Fold to the base using tabs C.
   For extreme asymmetry, make the main pop-up using Mechanism **31**, instead of **3**.
2. Stick tab D to E on the base.
3. Fold the double-triangle into its closed position and put glue on tab F.
4. Close the base so that tab F finds its natural glueing position, G.

28. THE M-FOLD

Multiple V-Folds can be made out of one piece of card.

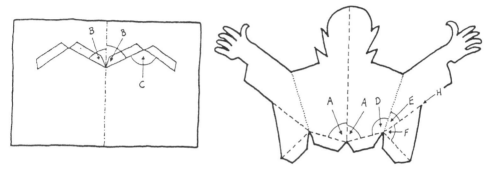

To draw up the most simple example of this, there are three rules:
1. Angles A are bigger than angles B. 2. Angle C, on the base, is the same as angle D, on the pop-up piece. 3. Angle E is the same as angle F.
Try angles: A = 65°; B = 45°; C = 115°; D = 115°; E = 45°; F = 45°.

To change the angles that straddle the spine, see Mechanisms **4** & **31**.

To adjust the outer planes of the pop-up, when crease H is a mountain fold:
To make angle C smaller than angle D: If D = C + x°, then E = F+x°.
Try angles: A=80°, B=60°, C=110°, D=130°, E=70°, F=50°.

To make angle C bigger than angle D. Where C = D+y°, then F = E+y°.
Try angles: A=80°, B=70°, C=130°, D=110°, E=60°, F=80°.

29.

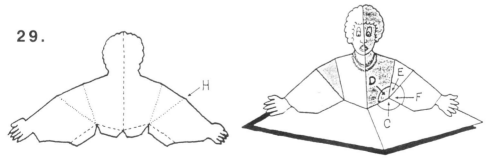

To adjust the outer planes of the pop-up, when crease H is a valley fold:
To make angle C smaller than angle D: If D = C+z°, then F = E+z°.
Try angles: A=80°, B=60°, C=95°, D=130°, E=40°, F=75° .

To make angle C bigger than D: When C = D+w°, then E = F+w°.
Try angles: A=70°, B=40°, C=70°, D=65°, E=85°, F=80°.

30. ASYMMETRICAL MOUTHS AND BEAKS

The asymmetrical movement of the mouth creates delightfully quirky characters. When the base is fully open the mouth pieces lie flat.

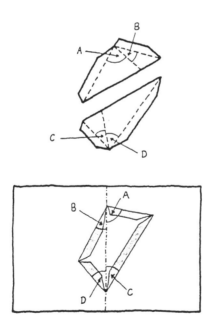

With these asymmetrical mechanisms there is a crucial rule:
When the angles between the sticking-strips and the spine do not match, the opposing angles on the page and the pop up piece must be balanced. Thus in this case: Angle A is the same on the top piece and on the base, angle B on the top piece is the same as B on the base. Similarly, angle C on the bottom piece matches C on the base, and D is the same on the bottom piece and the base.

31. ASYMMETRICAL SLOPING PLANES

This mechanism raises planes at wild and unexpected angles. The pop-up's central crease will lean towards the side of the base which has the larger angle between the sticking-strip and the spine, D in these examples.

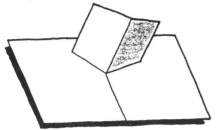 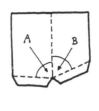 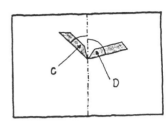

Angles A+B are always more than C+D. The amount that A is bigger than D, is the same as the amount that B is bigger than C. A = D + x; B = C + x.
e.g. D = 60°, C = 30°, x = 15°, then A = 75°, B = 45°.

The examples below are a guide to how different combinations of angles work. Remember that they can also be placed pointing backwards on the base.

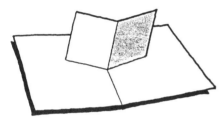 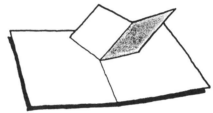

A=85°, B=65°, C=60°, D=80°.
Left and right hand planes both lean slightly backwards and to the right.

A=85°, B=35°, C=30°, D=80°.
Left and right hand planes both lean sharply backwards to the right.

A=130°, B=80°, C=30°, D=80°.
Left hand plane is almost vertical. Right hand plane leans forward.

A=100°, B=50°, C=30°, D=80°.
Left hand plane leans back slightly. Right hand plane is nearly vertical.

A=115°, B=95°, C=60°, D=80°.
Left and right hand planes both lean forwards and slightly to the right.

A=125°, B=55°, C=10°, D=80°.
Left hand plane leans hard to the right. Right hand plane leans sharply forward.

To find a specific angle of lean always take several experimental attempts.

32. SWIVELLING JAW

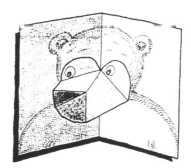

As the base opens the muzzle swings towards the larger angle on the base.

To construct this mechanism:-

1.   Start with the base.
Score the spinal crease, S, on base.

2.   At the desired angles, A & B, draw
the guide lines C & D that the tabs will
stick down against. The way angles A & B
work is explained in Mechanism **31.**

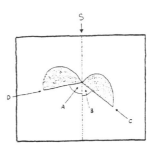

3.   On the pop-up piece draw, but don't
score, line E F, the central axis of the
pop-up piece.

4.   Draw and score lines E G, and E H.
Angle I = B + x, Angle J = A + x.

5.   Score the central axis, line E K.

6.   Draw and score lines K L, and K M.
They do not have to be at equal angles
to the axis line. The larger the angle
between KL and KM, the greater the bend
between the top and front of the muzzle.

7.   Measure angle N, this is the
angle between lines K M and K F.

8.   Draw and score line K P so that
the angle O is the same as angle N.
This crease, K P, forms the valley
fold down the front of the muzzle.

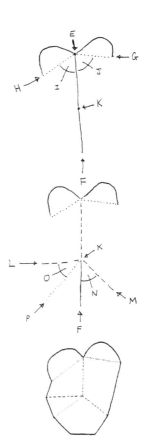

9.   Draw the edges of the pop-up piece.
Rub out the guide line K F. Cut out the
pop-up piece. Crease all the folds thoroughly.
Stick the pop-up to the base.

Try angles : A = 70°, B = 45°, I = 55°,
            J = 80°, N = 30°, O = 30°.

33. ASYMMETRICAL EXTENSIONS

The mechanism opposite can be extended to three tiers.

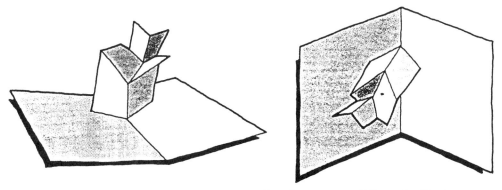

Using the base vertically or horizontally gives very different effects.

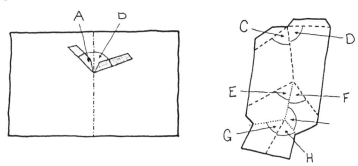

To construct a three tiered piece, treat line K P as the central axis line (see mechanism opposite), then repeat steps 6 to 9.

When extending Mechanism **32** in this way, pay special attention to the way the mountain and valley folds vary.

Try angles:
A = 45°, B = 70°, C = 60°, D = 85°, E = 50°, F = 70°, G = 50°, H = 70°.

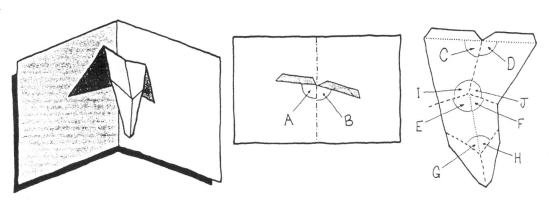

By making angle G less than 90°, the third stage can be made to bend back towards the base.

Try angles: A = 97°, B = 73°, C = 78°, D = 102°, E = 85°,
F = 60°, G = 45°, H = 45°, I = 120°, J = 85°.

34. THE PARALLELOGRAM

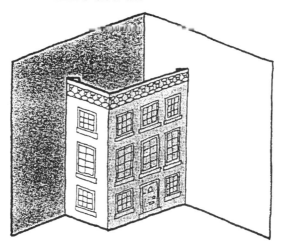

This is one of the basic building blocks of pop-up design. Although it can open out flat, in this case it is designed to be looked at with the base open at 90°.

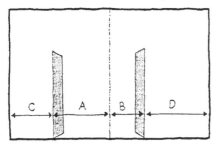

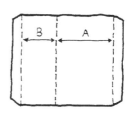

The two sticking strips lie parallel to the spine.

Length A on the base is the same as A on pop-up piece. Length B on the base is the same as B on the pop-up piece.

To prevent the pop-up jutting out when the base is closed make sure that length C is longer than B, and that D is longer than A.

Parallelograms can enclose others without touching them.

35.

A small parallelogram can be used as the "muscle" to raise a large image.

36. MULTIPLE PARALLELOGRAMS

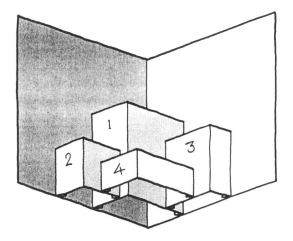

The mechanism can be extended by building parallelograms onto each other.

On piece1:
length A equals A on the base,
and length B equals B on the base.

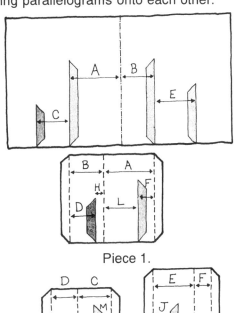

On piece 2:
length C equals C on the base,
and length D equals D on piece1.

Piece 1.

On piece 3:
length E equals E on the base,
and F equals F on piece1.

Working out the lengths for
piece 4 is a little more tricky.
Length G equals H on piece1+ J on piece 3.
Length K equals L on piece1+ M on piece 2.
To check these lengths there is another
way to look at it: D+G = B+J, and F+K = A+M.

Piece 2.   Piece 3.

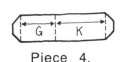

Piece 4.

Try:- A = 8 cm. B = 4 cm. C = 4 cm; D = 2 cm. E = 6 cm. F = 2 cm.
       G = 4 cm. H = 1 cm. J = 2 cm. K = 8 cm. L = 6 cm. M = 2 cm.

When designing, it's worth considering using the Quadrilateral (Mechanism
54), instead of the Parallelogram. Although closely related, the Quadrilateral
is asymmetrical and doesn't flatten out when the base is fully open.

37. PARALLELOGRAMS CUT FROM THE BASE

This mechanism doesn't use glue, however the scoring and cutting must be done very carefully. All the scored lines are parallel to the spine.

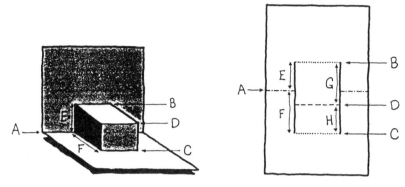

To construct the most basic parallelogram : 1. Draw, but don't score the spine line, A. 2. Above line A, draw and score line B. Length E will be the height of the parallelogram. 3. Below line A, draw and score line C. Length F will be the depth of the parallelogram. 4. Measure out the position of line D. Lengths G = F and H=E. Draw and score line D. 5. Make two vertical cuts joining the ends of lines B & C. 6. Score the two sections of line A that lie outside the cuts. 7. Push the parallelogram out. Crease D becomes a mountain fold while B and C become valley folds.

Parts of the planes can be made to jut upwards or backwards. Make sure you don't score the lines where the extensions join the plane.

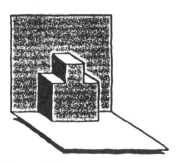

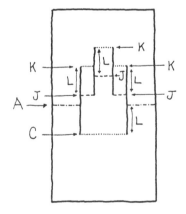

To make this variation :
1. Draw the spine line, A. 2. Draw line C. 3. Draw the front elevation onto line C, the lines J must be parallel to line C. 4. Draw the lines K. The lengths L, from J to K, are the same as L between A and C. 5. Score all the fold lines. Make the cuts. Ease the mechanism into its mountain and valley folds.

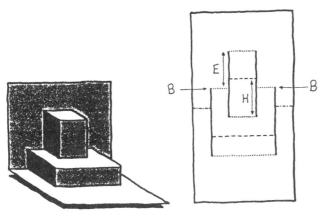
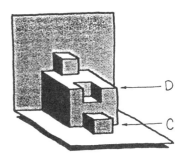

To vary the horizontal planes, receding steps can be added. Line B becomes the equivalent of a spine line, length E = H.

Lines C & D can also be modified as though they were spine lines.

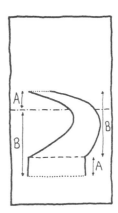

Non geometric shapes can be used, make sure that the measurements between creases is accurate.

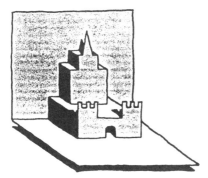
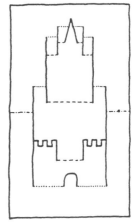

Try combining all the techniques.

When making these mechanisms, it's easiest to get a really clean result if all the drawing and scoring is done on the back of the card. When you come to do the scoring and cutting, remember: Score lines never cross Cut lines; and, Cut lines begin and end at Score lines.

38. PARALLELOGRAM STAND-UPS

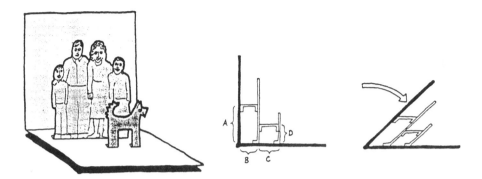

The base is used as both a floor and a background, small bridges pull up the pop-up images. Seen from the side the mechanism is a series of parallelograms: the bridges are horizontal and the image-pieces vertical. All the sticking-strips are parallel to the spine.

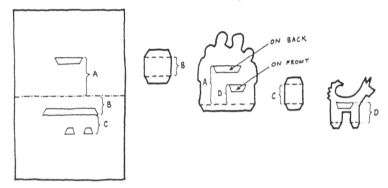

Length A on the base equals A on the back of the main pop-up piece. Length B on the base is the same as bridge 1. Length C on the base is the same as bridge 2. Length D on the back of the dog equals D on the main pop-up piece.

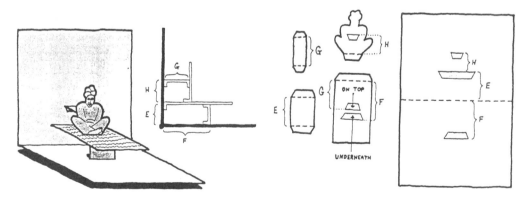

Here the main image-piece is horizontal, and the second, top one, is vertical. Length E on the base is the same as the E bridge. Length F on the base equals F on the underside of the carpet. Length G on top of the carpet is the same as the G bridge. Length H on the base equals H on the back of the figure.

39.   THE PARALLELOGRAM LIFTING V-FOLDS

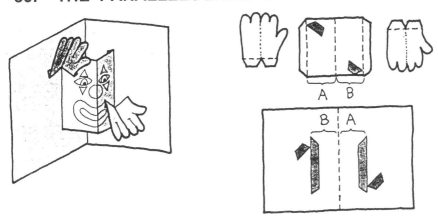

The gullies formed where a parallelogram joins the base can be used to raise V-Folds. Length A on the base equals A on the pop-up, similarly B equals B. To modify the pop-up angles of the face, see Mechanism **54**. To change the angles of the gloves, refer to Mechanisms **4** and **31**.

40.

With the base horizontal this mechanism can be used to pop-up images in the middle of the two pages. When the base is opened fully the parallelogram opens out flat, in effect its two sides become spine folds.

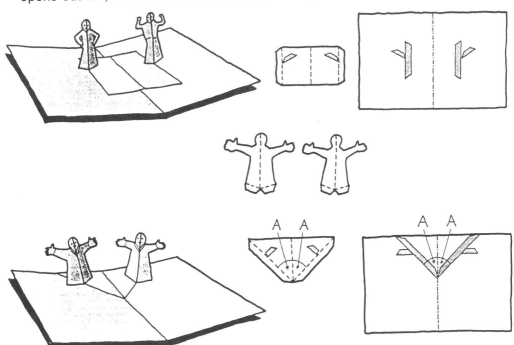

Here an extreme version of the V-Fold is used instead of a parallelogram. Making angles A all the same causes the V-Fold to open out flat. In practice, the large base triangle doesn't lie absolutely flat against the base, this can be disguised by positioning it so that its top edge is flush with the top of the base.

41. V-FOLDS LIFTING PARALLELOGRAMS

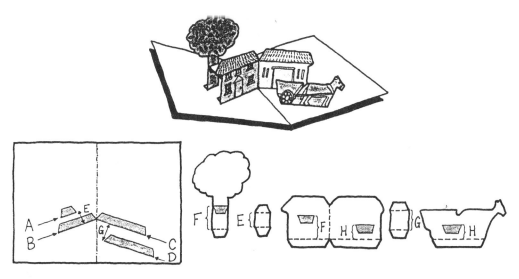

Here a simple V-Fold provides the muscle to pop-up other parallel planes. Sticking-strips B & C form the V-Fold, they are at the same angle to the spine. When adding the additional images, sticking-strip A must be parallel to B, and D must be parallel to C. These extra images are raised by small bridges that form parallelograms linking them to the V-fold. Bridge E is the same length as E on the base. F is the same both on the front of the tree and on the back of the building. Bridge G is the same length as G on the base, and height H is the same on the cart and on the front of the building.
Be careful: if the bridges are too narrow they buckle as the page opens.

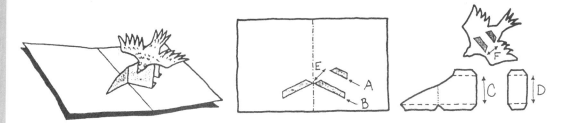

This mechanism can also be used to raise large planes parallel to the base. Sticking-strips A & B are parallel. The heights of the lifting-planes are the same, C equals D. Length E on the base equals F on the underside of the image.

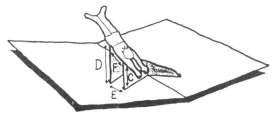

By using the Quadrilateral the image can be raised at an angle to the base, so that it slopes forwards. The key is to make E + D = C + F.
The Quadrilateral is explained in Mechanism **54**.

42.

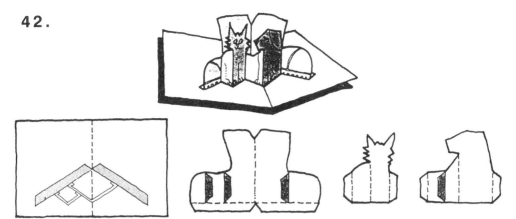

An array of parallelograms can be lifted by a simple V-Fold. The V-Fold is the only piece glued to the base, the parallelograms are stuck onto the front of the V-Fold. The plan view shows how the parallelograms are arranged.
This mechanism is a combination of **1** and **36**.

43.

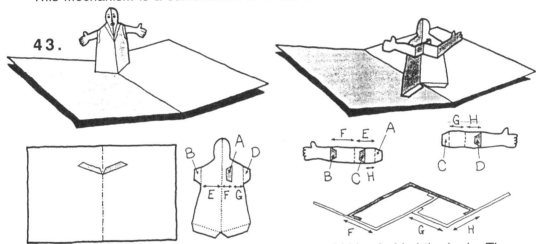

Here the arms are extensions of parallelograms hidden behind the body. The body is based on Mechanism **3**.   On arm 1: lengths E and F match E and F on the body.   On Arm 2: length G equals G on the body, and H equals H on arm 1.
If the arms are too low, or too long, they will clash with the base as it closes.

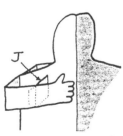

To make the arm stand forward from the figure, build a small parallelogram onto the front by adding piece J.

44. A more elegant, but tricky, version can be made by building the parallelogram onto Mechanism **28**.

45. ZIG-ZAG FOLDS

Two vertical valley folds A, and the central mountain fold, make the two central planes jut forward. The central section does not stick to the base.

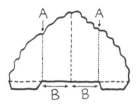
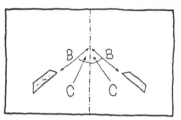

The vertical creases are all 90° to the bottom line of the pop-up piece. The two sticking-strips are the same distance from the spine, B & B. They are also at the same angle to it, C & C. To vary this one, lengths B on the pop-up piece can be longer than lengths B on the page.

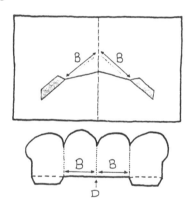

In this variation lengths B on the pop-up piece are shorter than lengths B on the base. The pop-up piece is symmetrical around line D.

46.

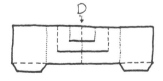
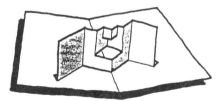

This design uses the same sticking positions on the base. It is also symmetrical around its vertical axis, D.

This mechanism has eight different pop-up planes, additional larger images can be stuck onto any of them.

47.

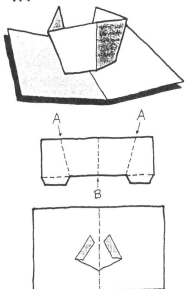
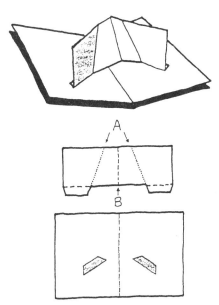

In these two variations the fold lines A are symmetrical on each side of the central crease B. The sticking strips also mirror each other on each side of the spine. By changing the angles of the fold lines and the positions of the sticking-strips many different shapes can be created, however, remember to keep them symmetrical.

48.

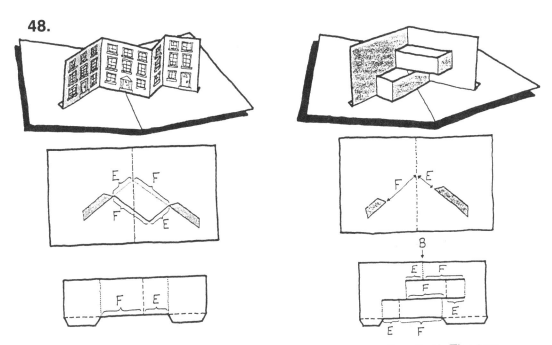

With both these designs the creases on the pop-up are all vertical. The two sticking-strips on the base are at the same angle to the spine. It is important that lengths E are the same on the pop-up and the base, the same applies to lengths F. In the design on the right B is the central crease.

49. POP-UP HOUSE

This rectangular house is based on a parallelogram raised by a V-Fold.

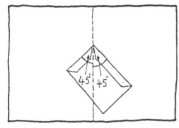
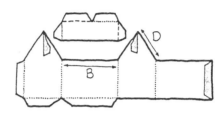
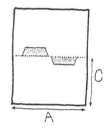

The sticking-strips are both 45° to the spine. The roof must overlap the walls or it will snag as the base closes. Length A is longer than B, and C is longer than D.

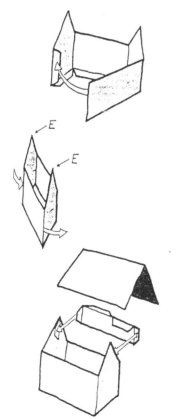

An elegant way of forming the four walls is to make them out of one long strip that "wraps around" to form a rectangle.

The roof cannot be attached to any of the walls, because as the page closes the walls' relationship to the roof changes. The only points on the walls that remain constant in relation to the roof are the two tips of the gable ends, marked E on the diagram.

The roof beam sticks to the two gable ends, it is parallel to the two long walls. The roof then sticks onto the two tabs on the top of the roof beam.

Suggested lengths : A = 7.5 cm. B = 6.5 cm. C = 4 cm. D = 3 cm.
Top of gable = 5.5 cm. above the base. Height of side walls = 3.5 cm.

50. PYRAMID

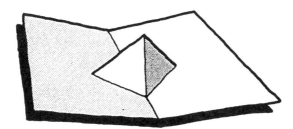

The two sticking strips are 45° to the spine. They can point either way, however the pyramid will look more solid on the base if they point forwards, towards the viewer.

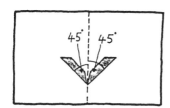 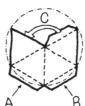

The easiest way to construct a pyramid is to start with a circle. The centre of the circle will be the apex of the pyramid. Having drawn the circle, measure out the lines of the pyramid's base along the circumference. Then add the two tabs for sticking the piece to the base, A & B, these must be on adjacent sides. Finally add tab C, this is used to pull it together.

 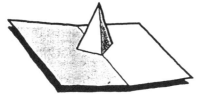 

Other pyramids:
To produce a tall narrow pyramid, make the sides of the base shorter than the radius of the circle.
To produce a low squat pyramid, make the sides of the base greater than the radius.
To produce a very low pyramid, two circles are necessary with two sides in each.
To place a pyramid squarely on the base, see Mechanism 52.

Pyramids are a useful pop-up mechanism. Big ones can be used as a starting point for other constructions. Small ones can be built into the gullies produced by other mechanisms.

51. TWO PARALLEL STICKING STRIPS

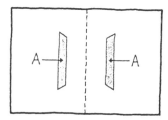

All the mechanisms on these two pages use the same pattern of sticking-strips on the base. The two sticking-strips, A, are equidistant from the spine and parallel to it. On all the designs tabs B stick onto A.

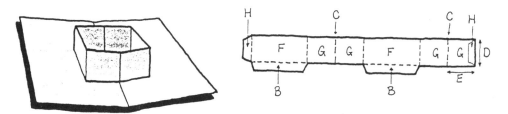

Creases C have to be vertical and above the spine.
If the design is too tall and narrow, length D is too long in relation to length E, planes F and G won't open fully. To cure this use pairs of small triangles as explained in Mechanism **80**.

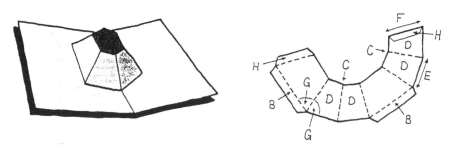

The shape of the pop-up can be varied as long as the mechanism remains symmetrical on each side of the spine. Creases C must always be directly above the spine. Tailor the bottom edges of planes D to make them fit the base. Try: Lengths B = 4 cm.; E = 4 cm.; F = 3.5 cm.; Angles G = 70°.

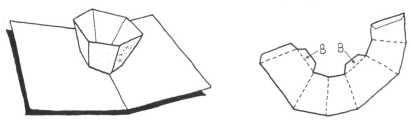

This pop-up shape can be stuck on either way up, just move tabs B.

52. SOLID SHAPES

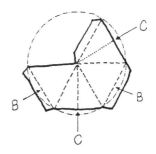

The glueing-tabs B that fix the pop-up to the page are on opposite sides of the pyramid. There are two creases C, these run down the centre of the two sides that straddle the spine, they can be either mountain or valley folds.

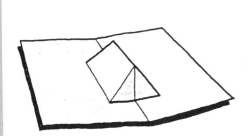
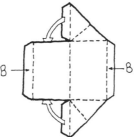
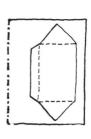

This is a stretched variation of the pyramid, the end creases are vertical.

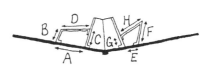

The sides of this mechanism can pull up additional images. Small bridges are used as shown in Mechanism **38**. The angle of the additions can be adjusted by using Mechanism **54**. The rule is: Lengths A+B = C+D, and E+F = G+H.

53.

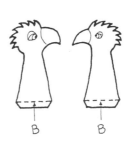

The most simple mechanism based on two parallel sticking-strips is made with two pieces of card. First glue the pop-up pieces back to back, then glue tabs B to the base.

54. QUADRILATERALS

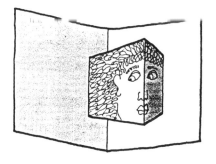
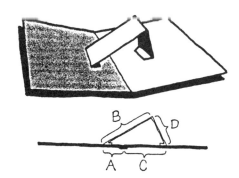

This is a very useful variation on the basic parallelogram. Unlike the parallelogram, this mechanism continues to jut out even when the base is opened out flat. Extensions can be added as shown in Mechanism **35**.

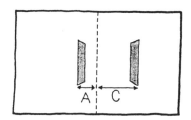
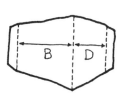

The two sticking strips that attach the pop-up piece to the base are parallel to the spine.
The total distance between the spine and the jutting out crease on the pop-up piece have to be equal on each side. This means that lengths A+B = C+D
Try: A = 2 cm. B = 8 cm. C = 6 cm. D = 4 cm.

55. To make the pop-up symmetrical length A = C, and B = D. Try lengths:
A = 4 cm. B = 3 cm. C = 4 cm. D = 3 cm.

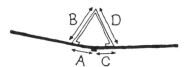

56.

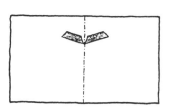
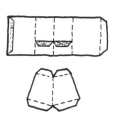

Instead of being glued directly to the base, a quadrilateral can be lifted above the page by a V-Fold. Mechanisms **10** and **22** explain ways of adjusting the angles on the lifting piece.

57. MULTIPLE QUADRILATERALS

This is a very versatile mechanism. Although it's important to get the lengths between the folds right, the height and shape of the various planes can all be different.

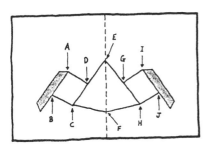

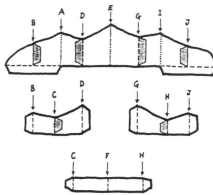

The two sticking-strips are the same distance from the spine and at the same angle to it.

For each quadrilateral the distance between the rear crease and the front crease must be balanced.

A B + B C = A D + D C

E C + C F = E H + H F

I G + G H = I J + J H

58.

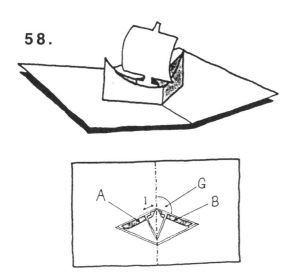

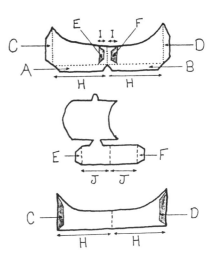

This boat is produced by combining three mechanisms. A V-Fold is the muscle which opens both a parallelogram forming the hull, and a quadrilateral which produces an interesting angle for the sail.

Suggested angles and lengths: G = 115°, H = 7 cm. I = 1.5 cm. J = 5 cm.

59. SLOT JOINTS

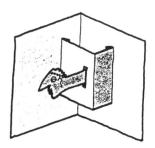

All these mechanisms use **slots**, they should be approximately 2mm. wide. These mechanisms are useful for making pieces jut out from the middle of a pop-up plane. This example can be built onto either a parallelogram, or a quadrilateral.

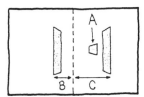 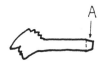

All the sticking-strips are parallel to the spine. The angle at which the head juts out can be varied by moving sticking-strip A nearer to, or further from, the spine. The slot D is parallel to the creases on the pop-up.

60.

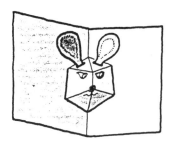

Here ears jut out of slots cut in an animal head based on Mechanism **15.**

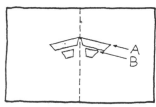 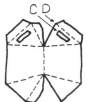

On the base, sticking-strip A is parallel to B.
On the pop-up piece, the slots C are parallel to the gluing tabs, D.
As the base closes the slots ride up the ear pieces; to allow them to move easily tailor the length of the slots and the width of the ears.

61.

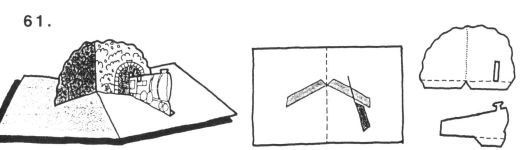

Here an extra piece juts forward from a vertical slot cut in a simple V-Fold. The extra piece is glued to the base in front of the V-Fold. As the base closes the extra piece folds down at a different angle to the V-Fold. To accommodate this make the top of the extra piece taper down behind the slot.

62.

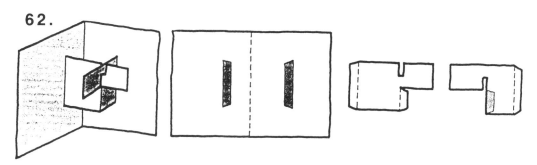

This mechanism shows how interlocking slots can be used to project both planes of a parallelogram. (See Mechanism **34**)

63.

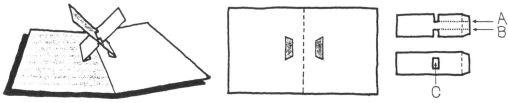

The two folds, A & B, are the key to this variation. Score the lines, but don't crease them firmly. Fold along A & B and then push them through slot C. Unfold them again, smooth them out, then stick the tab to the page.

The two mechanisms above can be adapted by using Mechanism **54**.

With added **3.**

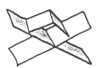

With added **55.**

With added **50.**

With added **63.**

Having glued the intersecting planes to the base, the central gully can be used, like a spine fold, to raise other mechanisms.

64.   V-FOLDS WITH JUTTING ARMS

The horizontal arms jutting forward from the figure are extensions of parallelograms hidden behind a V-Fold.

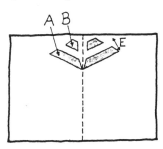
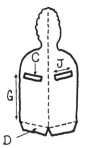
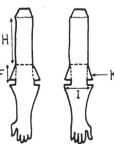
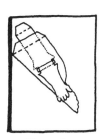

Closed

On the base, the sticking-strips A & B are parallel.
On the V-Fold, the slot C is parallel to tab D.
Length E on the base is the same as length F on the arm.
Length G on the body equals length H on the arm.

To hold the arms in position:
The arm is wider than the slot , I is bigger than J. Behind the slot the arm has two little tabs K; these are folded down as the piece is fed through the slot, then unfolded again to hold the arm in place. Do this before gluing the tab at the bottom of the arm to the base!

If you'd prefer the arms to project at a different angle, use the quadrilateral principle: E + G = F + H.

Other images can be added to the arms, use parallelograms and small bridges as explained in Mechanism **38**.

65.

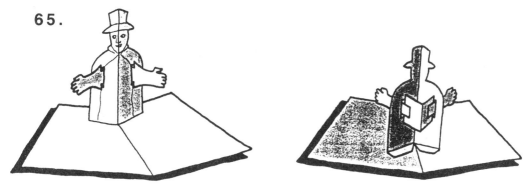

The vertical arms jutting forward from the figure are extensions of a quadrilateral suspended behind a V-Fold.

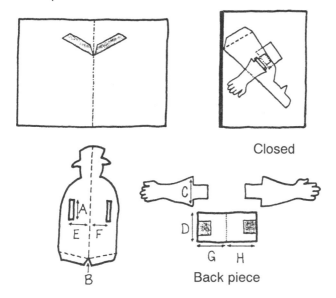

Closed

Back piece

The slots A are parallel to centre fold B, and the same distance from it.
The arms are wider than the slot, both C and D are larger than A.
To make the quadrilateral: lengths E = F and G = H.

To change the angle of the arms, make the lengths E + G = F + H.

66.

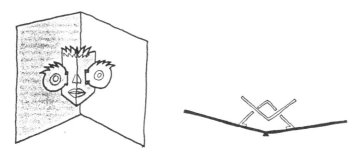

The same jutting mechanism can be combined with a parallelogram or a quadrilateral that is attached to the base.

67.   THE BASIC BOX

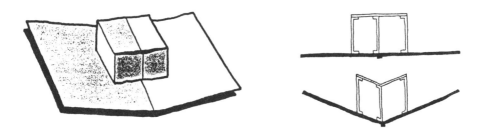

This mechanism is the basis of many "solid" pop-up designs. In essence it is made of two identical parallelograms that straddle the spine. The central piece is crucial, it pushes up the lid which in turn pushes out the top of the sides.

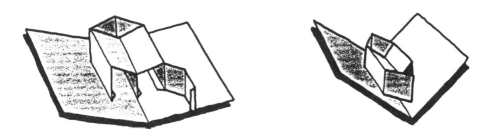

As the base closes, planes F fold outwards and the lid folds down.
The end planes, F, are important, they "lock" the mechanism upright and prevent it from leaning when the base is open.

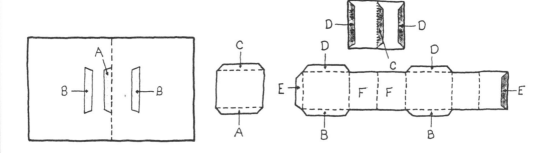

To build the box onto the base:
Start by sticking the central piece to the spine with tab A. Then stick tabs B, the sticking-strips B are parallel to and equidistant from the spine. Next stick the top of the central piece to the centre of the lid C. Stick the edges of the lid to the top of the sides using tabs D. Finally close the box using tab E.

68. CYLINDER

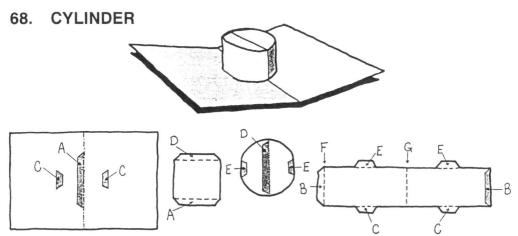

The rectangular box can be adapted to make a pop-up cylinder. The shape and position of the centre piece remains the same. Tabs C and E are about a quarter of the length of tab A. Creases F and G both stand vertically above the spine. To construct the cylinder follow the alphabetic gluing order indicated on the diagram.

When making this mechanism the lid may need to be trimmed so that it can fold down smoothly inside the cylinder as the base is closed.

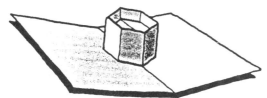

The hexagon works in the same way as the cylinder. It has six vertical creases, two of which must be above the spine. The two sides should be symmetrical. The lid does not have to be flush with the top of the sides. Useful effects are produced with a slightly sunken lid.

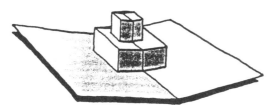

The lids of these boxes can be used as a base for further pop-ups. The central crease works like a spine fold.

When building these extensions, check where the pieces fold away to.

69.

A small quadrilateral (see Mechanism 55) is an alternative way of making the central support. This creates a firm plane above the page without the need for end pieces (F in Mechanism 67) to hold it steady when the base is open.

70. AEROPLANE

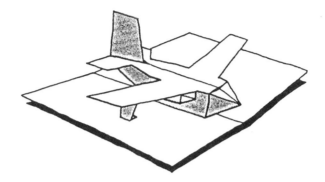

The box, explained in Mechanism **67**, can be used to make spectacular pop-up models. To build the pop-ups on these two pages follow the alphabetical gluing order shown in the diagrams. In this example the slot R and tail fins S, T, U will all have to be tailored to fit away as the base closes and the mechanism folds up.

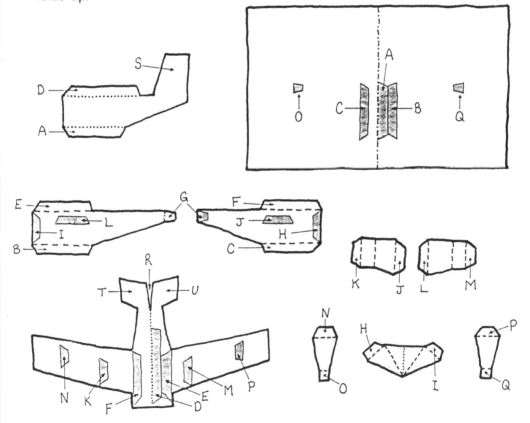

When making your own designs there are two key principles to remember:
1. Any pieces which cross the spine must have a fold directly above the spine. This applies both to pieces that stand up, straddling the spine; and to horizontal pieces that "float" above the base.
2. When building out from the spine, across the base, follow the parallelogram principle explained in Mechanism **38**.

71.

The creases for tabs D and E must be straight. The waterline between the ends of these tabs and the spine will have to be tailored to fit neatly against the base. Similarly the edges of the deck will need to be adjusted to make it fit easily within the hull. To get these right it will be necessary to make an experimental one first.

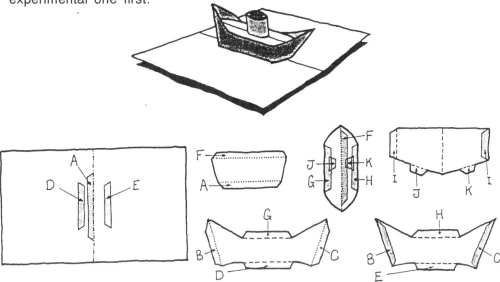

72.

This design can be adapted into many different animal forms. Getting the shapes right on the pieces that make the head and neck is very tricky. It will always be necessary to make at least one rough first in order to get the shapes, lengths, and angles right.

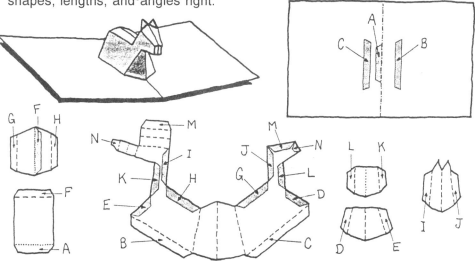

To vary the angles on the sides and top, use the quadrilateral principle, Mechanism **54**. In this case the distance from the spine to F to H, must be the same as from the spine to B to H.

73. SIMPLE MOVING ARM

This mechanism uses the 45° Fold. A small double-triangle is the muscle which lifts a larger moving image. The large image rises and falls as the base is opened and closed.

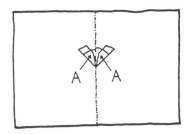 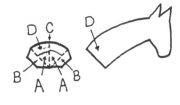

The angles A, on the base and on the double-triangle, are all 45° .
Stick the double-triangle to the base using tabs B.
Close the base, make sure that the central crease C folds forwards.
Open the base again, then stick the moving image to the small triangle on the left D, so that it juts out over the right hand page.

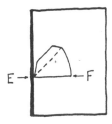 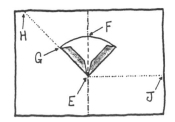

Base closed   Base open

The movement is generated by crease E F moving from a horizontal position when the base is closed, to a vertical position when the base is open.

The shape of the moving image can vary considerably. However when the base is open an image glued to triangle E F G must fit above the lines H E and E J.

THE SIMPLE ARM'S MOVEMENTS

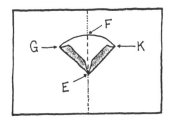

Although there are only two moving planes E F G and E F K, it's still possible to produce a wide range of effects. The moving image can project in four possible directions: to the left or right from E F, upwards from F G or F K.

| Closed | Opening | Open |

As the base opens, images projecting from the top, F G, move backwards; images projecting from the front, E F, move upwards.

If the double-triangle is placed pointing upwards the movement is reversed.

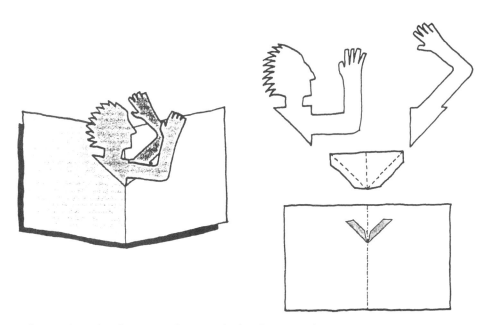

Several projections can be used simultaneously.
The shape of the arm affects the visual result: an arm with an elbow appears to move more than a straight arm.

74. 45° FOLDS ON A PARALLELOGRAM

A small double-triangle can be built onto the forward jutting corner of a parallelogram by adding two 45° folds. Moving images can then be glued onto the small triangles. Large movements can be created because the triangles that generate the action are distanced from the spine by the parallelogram.

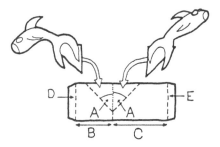

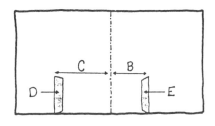

Both the angles A are 45°. Lengths B on the base and on the pop-up piece are equal, as are lengths C. Stick the parallelogram to the base using the tabs D and E, then stick the moving images onto the two small triangles.

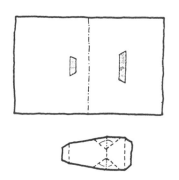

The 45° folds can be at the top or bottom of the parallelogram. Using both, like this, can create very exciting effects.

Stick the parallelogram to the base first. Close the base and press it firmly to establish the mountain and valley folds. Then open the base again and add the arms and legs.

Make a rough of this one to check where the legs and arms fold away to, they may need adjusting.

THE DIFFERENT MOVEMENTS

As the base opens and closes the images attached to the two small triangles move in two different ways. This is because the triangles are set in a parallelogram with a long side and a short side. In contrast, Mechanism **73** is symmetrical so the movement of the arms on each side mirror each other.

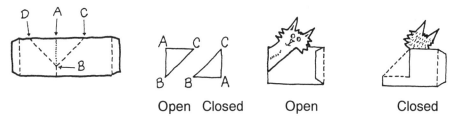

Open Closed   Open   Closed

The triangle A B C, on the long side of the parallelogram, flips over along the axis line B C. As the base opens and closes both sides of the stuck-on image are revealed.

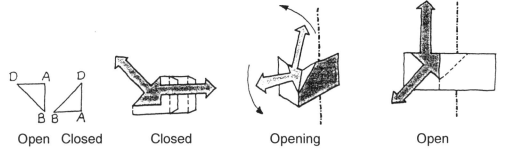

Open Closed   Closed   Opening   Open

The triangle A B D, on the short side of the parallelogram, rotates around point B. Only one side of an image stuck onto it is revealed. An arm jutting up from side A D will rise away from the spine, sliding across the page. An arm jutting from side D B will sink downwards, however only one side of the image is revealed.

With this version a masking piece can be stuck onto the front of the long side of the parallelogram to hide the lifting mechanism.

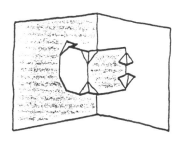

45° folds can be added to the jutting edge, or the gullies, formed by a parallelogram. For even more variations in movement, Mechanism **73** can be added to the gullies.

75. ARMS MOVING BEHIND A MASK

These two pages show how to make an image swing across the base in any direction. The source of the movement is hidden by the mask.

The mechanism is derived from the parallelogram, it is made with a long masking piece and a short, angled, hinge. The moving image is glued to the hinge. Length A on the hinge equals A on the base.

Note the difference between the mountain and valley folds on the clockwise and anti clockwise mechanisms.

To construct this mechanism:
1. Stick tab B on the mask to the base, then swing the mask out of the way to the left.
2. Stick the arm to the hinge, C. Pay special attention to which side of the hinge the arm glues to.
3. Put glue on the back of tab D and stick the hinge to the base.
4. Using the guide under each diagram, put the hinge into the correct position when the base is open.
5. Put glue on the front of tab E. Then with the base still open, swing the mask into position so that tab E finds its natural sticking position on the back of the mask. Length F on the base is the same as F on the back of the mask.

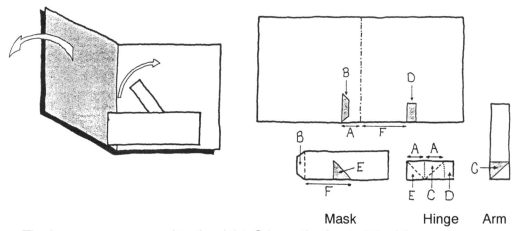

Mask　　　　　　　　Hinge　　　Arm

The image moves up and to the right. C is on the front of the hinge.
The hinge is flat when the base is open, and folded when the base is closed.

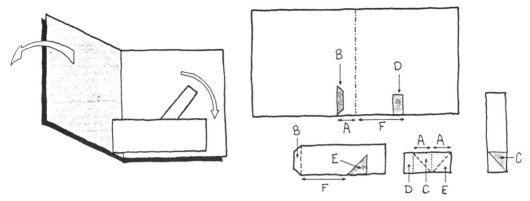

The image moves down and to the right. C is on the front of the hinge.
The hinge is folded when the base is open, and flat when the base is closed.

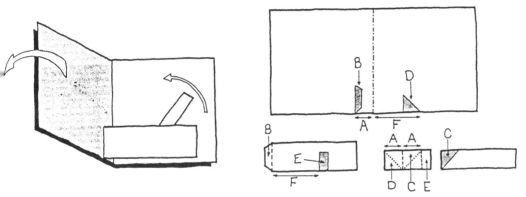

The image moves up and to the left. C is on the back of the hinge.
The hinge is folded when the base is open, and flat when the base is closed.

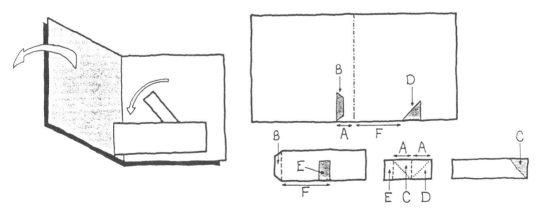

The image moves down and to the left. C is on the back of the hinge.
The hinge is flat when the base is open, and folded when the base is closed.

This mechanism is well worth experimenting with.

76. A TURNING DISC

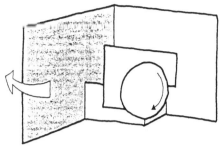 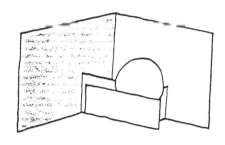

As the base opens the disc rotates. A pair of small triangles are folded into the forward jutting edge of a basic parallelogram. An L-shaped piece attached to one of the triangles transmits movement to the disc.

A and B are parallel to the spine.
Length C is the same on the base
and on the parallelogram.
Lengths D are also equal.

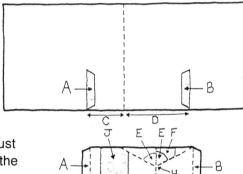

On the parallelogram the angles E must
be the same. The larger the angles E the
more the disc will turn.
If E = 60° the disc will turn through 120°.

One arm of the L-shaped piece, F, sticks to the
triangle on the short side of the parallelogram, F.
The other arm sticks to the disc G.

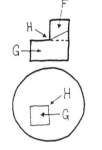

It is important that the three points H are
aligned exactly on top of each other.
On the disc, H is the centre point.

When the base closes and the parallelogram
folds shut the disc will tend to lean backwards.
To keep the disc upright an extra piece is
added to the long side of the parallelogram.

The extra piece can be either type J
which goes behind the top of the disc
(top left diagram). Or it can be type K
which goes in front of the bottom of the
disc (top right diagram).

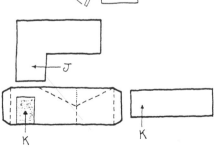

This extra piece can be strengthened by
making it into a parallelogram.

CLOCKWISE AND ANTICLOCKWISE MOVEMENT

The diagrams below show how to obtain movement in either direction whether the long side of the parallelogram is on the right or the left of the base.

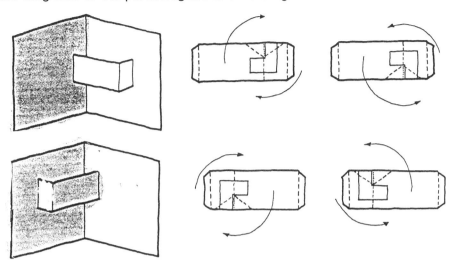

The direction of the disc's rotation can be reversed by changing the position of the double triangle. The L-shaped piece always sticks to the small triangle on the short side of the parallelogram.

CAR WITH TWO TURNING WHEELS

To make the car's two wheels turn as the base is opened; start with a double parallelogram as shown in the diagram above right.

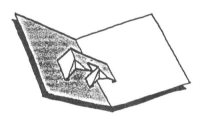

The car's body sticks on last, it stops the wheels leaning forwards as the base closes.

Accuracy is important.
Try lengths: A = 8.5 cm. B = 2 cm. C = 2 cm. D = 6.5 cm.

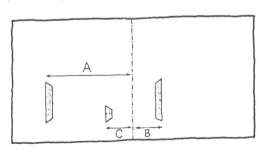

77. THE DOUBLE 45° FOLD

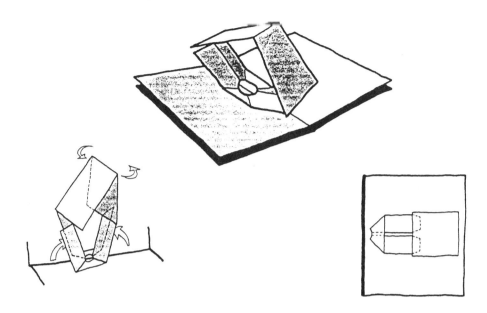

Closed

This is an intriguing mechanism, which produces a very unusual movement; as the base closes the two arms rise while the top piece twists around.

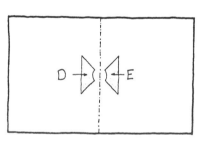

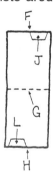

Making the arms:

Each of the four angles A is 45°.

The four valley-folds B, all meet at the central point C.

To reduce the thickness of the folded card at this central point, remove a circular hole from around C.

Having thoroughly creased all the fold lines, open the piece out flat and stick areas D and E to the base.

Making the top piece:

It is important that the length of the top piece, F G H, is longer than the length of the arms F C H.

When sticking the top piece onto the top of the arms it is important to attach it diagonally, I sticks to J and K sticks to L.

This is an interesting mechanism to develop as it has six planes to play with. When making your own designs, the pop-up can be made asymmetrical. The key is to think of it as a quadrilateral, then lengths C F + F G = C H + H G.

78. JACK IN THE BOX

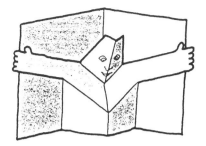

This mechanism uses two pairs of 45° folds on an adapted parallelogram. The surprising aspect of this design is that when the base is open the arms can reach out beyond its edges.

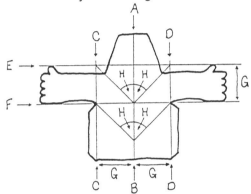

Start by drawing, but not scoring, the guide lines.
The pop-up piece is symmetrical around the central line A B.
Lines C and D are parallel to A B.
Lines E and F are at 90° to line A B, and are parallel to each other.
The length G, is the same between all these parallel lines.
The angles H are all 45°.

When drawing the figure onto the guide lines make sure that the arms do not extend above line E, if they do they will clash with the spine as the base closes. The arms can be extended below line F.

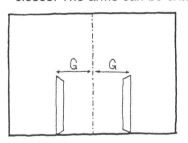

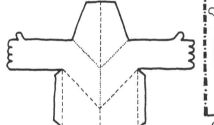

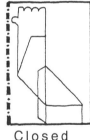

Closed

Score the fold lines marked, then rub out the guide lines and cut out the pop-up piece. Thoroughly crease all the mountain and valley folds before sticking the pop-up to the base. The two sticking-strips are parallel to the spine.

79.

This variation uses the same arrangement of two pairs of 45° folds, but here they are incorporated into a V-Fold instead of a Parallelogram.

(Compare with Mechanism **33**.)

80. STRUCTURAL USES OF 45° FOLDS

This pop-up doesn't have to be centrally placed on the base.

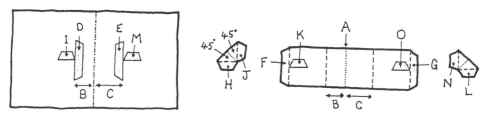

When the base is open valley fold A must be exactly above the spine, therefore lengths B and C on the pop-up equal B and C on the base. The sticking-strips D and E must be parallel to the spine. Having glued the main piece to the base (F to D and G to E), add the pairs of 45° folds, stick H to I and J to K, L to M and N to O. Make sure that I is at 90° to D, and K is at 90° to F.

81. A pair of 45° folds can pull up a single sheet of card rising from the spine. The angles A are all 45°. The base is the same for both these designs.

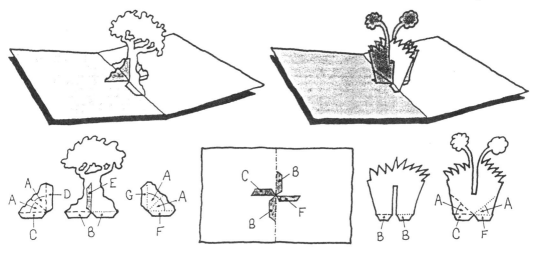

First stick tabs B to the base. Then stick tab C to the base and tab D to E on the front of the tree. Stick tab F to the base, then stick G to position E on the back of the tree.

This adaptation uses interlocking slots that allows the piece at right-angles to the spine to extend upwards. The slots should be 2mm. wide. Stick tabs C and F to the base first, then stick tabs B.

82. BOX ENDS

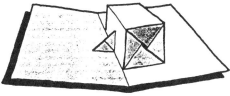

Here one double 45° fold is used to pull up a box. The box is a parallelogram with one side lying along the spine. Two more double 45° folds are used to fill in the end of the box.

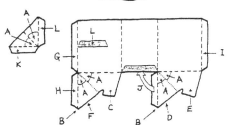 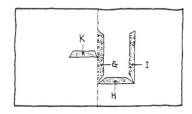

The angles A are 45°. Lines B are angled to run diagonally from corner to corner across the end of the box. C and D are extensions that jut behind their opposing edges C behind E and D behind F, these ensure that there is no gap in the end when the base is open. Stick the box to the base using tabs G, H and I, then close the end by sticking Tab J. Finally, add the double 45° fold by sticking K and L. Make sure that K and L are wide enough to take the strain as the base opens.

Without the adapted triangles that fill in the end the single triangle K L won't pull up the parallelogram. These end pieces must be attached to the sides of the box that come together as the parallelogram closes.

83.

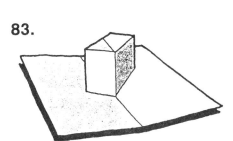 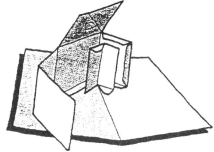

The box's lid is lifted by a strut using the parallelogram principle.

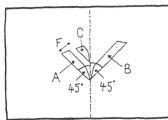 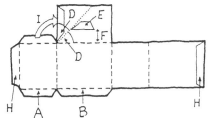

On the base: sticking-strips A and B are both 45° to the spine, sticking-strip C is parallel to A. On the box lid: angles D are both 45°, sticking-strip E is parallel to the crease between the lid and the top of the side. Length F on the lid equals F on the base. Strut height G equals the height of the sides.

To make the box, stick the tabs in this order: A, B, C, E, H, I. Finally close the base and press firmly to make sure that the last tab sticks securely.

84. THE BASIC PULL-STRIP

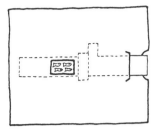 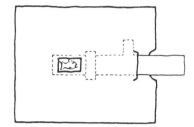

The movement in all these interactive mechanisms is generated by the viewer pulling a pull-strip. This slide is the most simple of these mechanisms, its components; the pull-strip, tab, slit and sleeve are used in all of them.
In this example, pulling the strip causes an image to change behind a window in the base. The lengths, and the positions of the tab and the sleeve have to be carefully worked out.

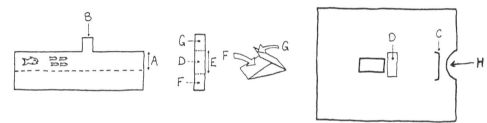

The Pull-strip: Make pull-strips double thickness to prevent them buckling when they're pushed. The strongest way of making the strip is to score it along its length, then fold it over, and stick the two sides back to back. The width of the strip is A, try A = 2cm. When drawing up the strip, remember to include the tab on one side.

The Tab: B in diagram. When the strip is pulled the movement is stopped by the tab coming up against slit C; when it is pushed it stops when the tab comes up against the sleeve D.

The Slit: C in diagram. This is a simple cut in the base which the pull-strip passes through. It should be about 4mm. wider than the pull-strip (length A). The ends of the slit curve backwards about 3mm., this enables one side of the slit to lift slightly and allows the strip to move more easily.

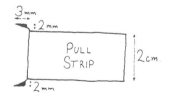

The Sleeve: D in diagram. The sleeve guides the strip and holds it flush with the base. Length E is 3mm. longer than A. To make the sleeve: F folds over D, then G folds over and sticks to F. Finally stick D to the back of the base. If the sleeve is too tight or too loose the strip can jam.

The Base: Taking a bite, H, out of the side of the base makes gripping the pull-strip easier. To protect and hide the mechanism another sheet of card can be fixed to the back, stuck on around the edges of the base.

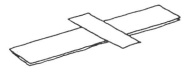

Quick Tab.

Usually the tab is an integral part of the strip. When making roughs it's often easiest to find the right position for the tab by sticking a piece of card across the pull-strip.

Quick Sleeve.

A small piece of card can be used to make a simple sleeve. Cut a slit in the card and stick the shaded area A, to the page.

Other ways of controlling pull-strips are shown in Mechanisms **86** and **89**.

85. LARGE SLIDE

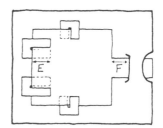

The pull-strip moves a sheet of card behind the base, this causes the images behind several windows to change simultaneously.

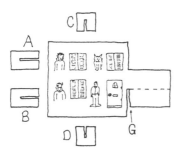

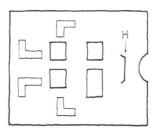

The moving sheet is guided and held flush to the base by four small pieces of card A, B, C, D, these are cut so that they have two arms. One arm sticks to the back of the base, the other arm holds the edge of the moving sheet in place. Length E on arms A and B must be more than length F on the pull-strip.

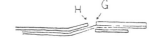

For a pull-strip to slide smoothly, edges must not clash. Here the pull-strip's double thickness is made by folding the extra piece underneath. If it is folded on top, the edge G will snag against slit H when the strip is pushed in.

86. THROUGH THE PAGE SLIDES

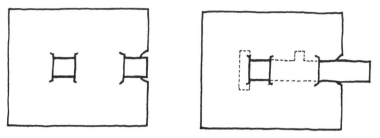

A simple way to guide the pull-strip is to weave it through three parallel slits in the page.

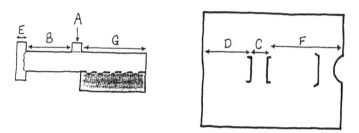

To construct this slide: fold tab A over, thread the pull-strip through the slits, then unfold the tab again. The lengths are important: B should be at least double length C; D should not be less than B + E; F equals G + A.

The woven slide doesn't have to be a simple narrow strip, the image section can be made much wider.

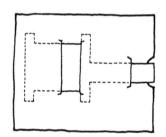

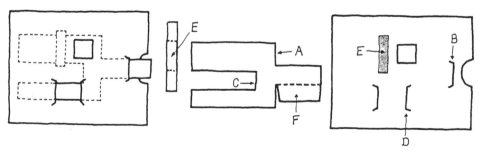

The pull-strip can be divided into arms using both the woven slide and the sleeve guided slide. The movement is controlled by edge A coming up against slit B, and edge C coming up against slit D. In this example sleeve E holds the upper arm to the back of the page. Fold strengthening-piece F underneath, see Mechanism **85.**

87. EXTENDING THE IMAGE

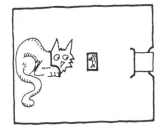 

As the strip is pulled, the image extends across the page.

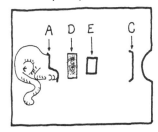 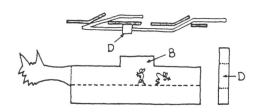

The strip folds back on itself and pokes through a slit in the page, A. The movement is limited by the long tab B meeting slit C when pulled and sleeve D when pushed. The sleeve D also holds the strip flush with the page. The small window E allows an extra image to change as the strip is pulled.

A large image can be stuck onto the moving end of the extending piece, this glides across the page as the strip is pulled and also completely hides slit A.

88. THE INVISIBLE GUIDE

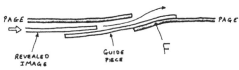

When the strip is pulled the image suddenly "appears from nowhere"!
An extra piece of card is used to guide the hidden image through the slit and into view. The guide-piece sticks to the front of the page at F and extends under the page through the slit.

DELAYED REVEALED IMAGE

When the strip is pulled, the image behind the window starts changing. Near the end of the movement the revealed image suddenly appears. The key to this mechanism is the long guide-piece.

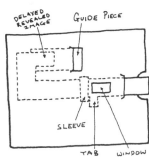

89. SLOT GUIDED SLIDE

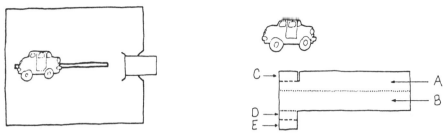

A slot 2 mm. wide acts as a guide rail for the pull-strip, no sleeve is needed.

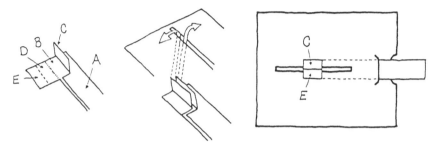

To construct the pull-strip: Glue the pull-strip back to back, A sticks to B, then fold tab C into an upright position. Fold D over and stick it to B, then fold E into an upright position.

With the strip beneath the page push C and E up through the slot, then fold them out flat on top of the page, one on each side of the slot. Finally, stick the moving image onto C and E.

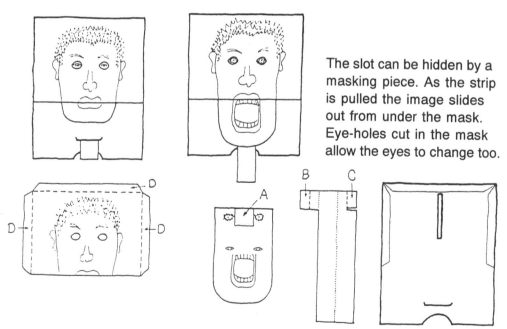

The slot can be hidden by a masking piece. As the strip is pulled the image slides out from under the mask. Eye-holes cut in the mask allow the eyes to change too.

A, on the underside of the image, sticks to B and C on the pull-strip. Stick the mask to the edges of the page using gluing tabs D.

90. KNEE MECHANISM

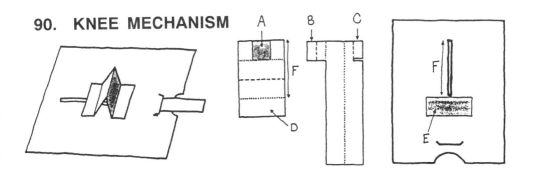

The slot-guided slide can be used to raise a knee mechanism.
To construct the knee: A sticks to tabs B and C, D sticks to E on the base. It's important that length F on the base equals F on the knee piece.

91. MOVING IMAGE BEHIND A V-FOLD

Here a slot-guided slide moves a vertical image behind a V-Fold.

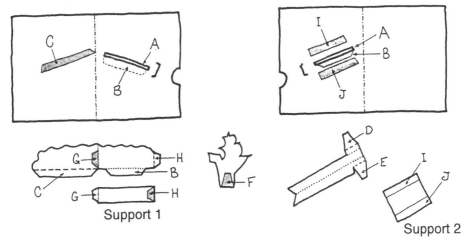

Support 1

Support 2

To construct this mechanism:
Decide on the angles of the V-Fold's sticking-strips, see Mechanism **2**. Cut slot A along the line of sticking-strip B. Tab B goes through the slot, folds forward and sticks to the underside of the base. Stick Tab C into position on the top side of the base. Make the pull-strip in the same way as opposite. Push tabs D and E up through slot A. They remain vertical and are glued onto each side of tab F. Stick support 1 into place using tabs G and H, this holds up the moving image and stops it flopping down backwards. Support 2 keeps the pull-strip up against the base, stick tabs I and J.

92. WOVEN DISSOLVE

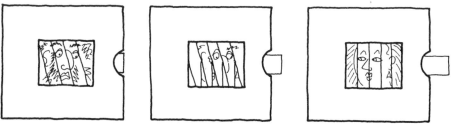

Pulling the strip causes one image to dissolve into another.
Very accurate measuring and smooth cutting are essential with this design.

Grid lengths:
A = 4 cm.
B = 1.5 cm.
C = 2 cm.
D = 1 cm.
E = 7 cm.

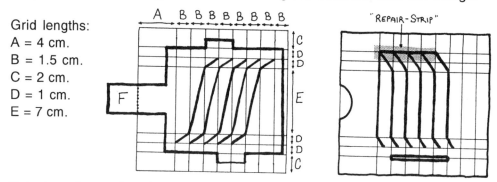

Take two pieces of card, one to make the slide and the other the base. Draw an identical grid of guide lines on the back of each one. Then follow the pattern of cuts shown in the diagrams above. On the base there are six vertical slits, on the slide there are five slits which are all approximately 10° off vertical. All the slits have an angled "tail-section" at each end. Pay special attention to the different ways the angles on the "tail-sections" fit onto the grids. On the base a horizontal cut along the top of the slits turns them into strips. These are threaded up through the slits in the slide, one strip through each slit. When the slide has been positioned, smooth the top of the base-strips down so that they lie flush with the base, then repair the horizontal cut with a strip of tape or a patch of card.

Back view

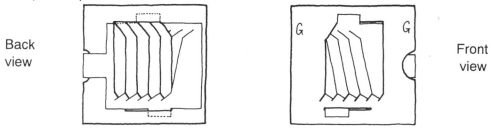

Front view

The bottom of the slide lies behind the base with the tab projecting down through the slot. The top of the slide lies in front of the base's panel of slits.

It's important that both pieces stay rigid when the tab is being pushed and pulled. To strengthen the slide make the pull-tab double thickness, fold over extension F shown in the diagram. To strengthen the base and hide the interlocking ends of the strips: stick a masking piece with a window onto the front, the gluing areas for this are on the sides of the base, G. A backing sheet can also be added, this sticks to the top and bottom edges of the base.

93. PANEL DISSOLVE

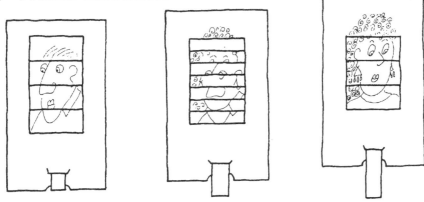

Each of the two pictures is made of four panels. The panels on the moving section are attached to a long pull-strip.

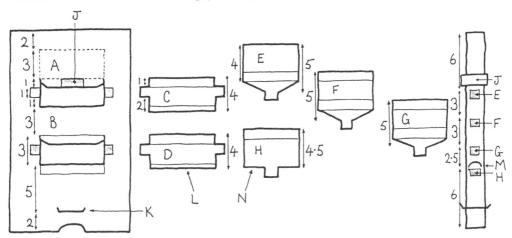

On the page the panels A and B are integral to the base. The other two panels, C and D, are additional pieces that are stuck into place across windows cut in the base. The top of each of these sections also slightly overlaps the bottom of the panel above it.

When making this mechanism, accurate measuring is vital.
Start by constructing the base: stick pieces C and D into place on the back of the base using the tabs at the side. The top of each piece lies on the front of the base; the bottom of each piece lies behind the base.

To construct the pull-strip: starting at the top, stick piece E to the front of the strip, then add piece F so that its top edge overlaps the bottom edge of piece E, repeat with pieces G and H.

To assemble the mechanism: start by sliding the top of the strip through the sleeve J on the back of the base. Thread piece E up under the top cut in the base, then F under piece C, G under the second cut in the base, H under piece D. Finally thread the bottom of the strip through slit K. A backing sheet can be added if desired.

Up movement stops when L meets M; down movement stops when N meets K.

94. FLAP LIFTS AWAY FROM PULL-STRIP

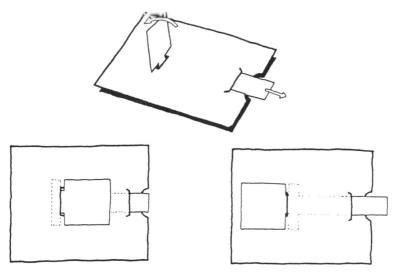

Pulling the pull-strip causes a hidden mechanism to lift a flap and flip it over. At its most simple an image underneath the flap is revealed.

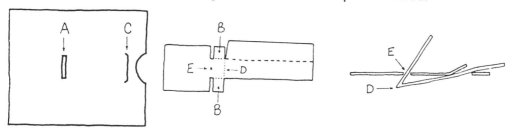

Slot A is 2mm. wide. It works as a fulcrum, the flap is levered up by pulling the strip. To assemble the mechanism: Fold over tabs B and feed the strip, including the tabs, through the slot. Flatten the tabs out again and push the end of the strip through slit C. The distance between fold D and point E is 7mm. The stress is at point E. To prevent it from bending it can be strengthened with a patch of card.

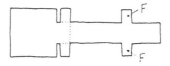

To raise the flap up but stop it from flipping right over, add a pair of tabs F. When these meet slit C they stop the pull movement.

Flaps can be combined with many pop-up mechanisms. As the flap lifts, it raises a pop-up structure. The gully formed between the flap and the base is used as a spine-fold. V-Folds, parallelograms, and moving arms can be built onto it. See Mechanisms **99** and **100** for examples.

95. FLAP LIFTS TOWARDS THE PULL-STRIP

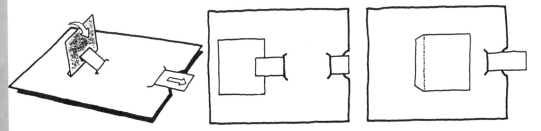

The pull-strip emerges from the page and pulls up the flap.

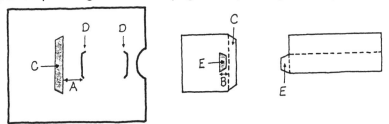

It's important to make length A on the base longer than length B on the flap. Make length B approximately 1cm. Start by sticking tab C to the base, then thread the strip through slits D. Finally stick tab E onto the flap.

96. DECK CHAIR FLAP

This mechanism uses a slot joint to pull up two planes at different angles.

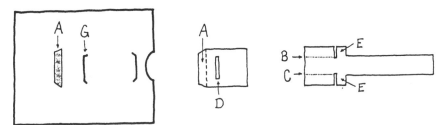

Start by sticking tab A to the base. Then fold the broad end of the strip at B and C, push it through slot D, then flatten B and C out again. The tabs E stop the strip sliding too far.

The length F, between tabs E and slit G, is critical. Making F small limits the amount that the flaps can lift. If F is large the top flap flips right over.

97. TWO FLAPS LIFTED BY ONE PULL-STRIP

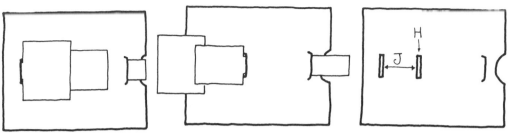

These flaps are based on Mechanism **94**. Tab G goes through slot H and sticks to the pull-strip. Make sure that length J between the slots on the base equals J on the pull-strip. K equals 7 mm., both on the pull-strip and on the second flap.

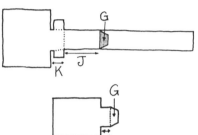

For a delayed-action variant of this, see Mechanism **101**.

98.

These flaps, linked in a chain, are based on Mechanism **95**.

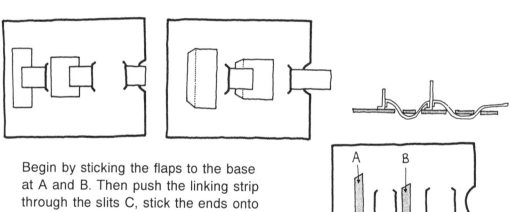

Begin by sticking the flaps to the base at A and B. Then push the linking strip through the slits C, stick the ends onto the flaps, D to D and E to the back of F. Push the main pull-strip through the slits G, then stick H to the front of F.

Space the flaps and slits carefully to avoid sticking-points and slits clashing.

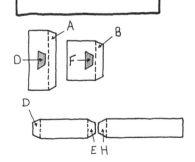

99. FLAPS LIFTING POP-UPS

 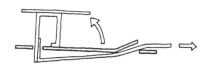

A parallelogram is built onto a flap, then a leaping image is attached to the top of the parallelogram.

 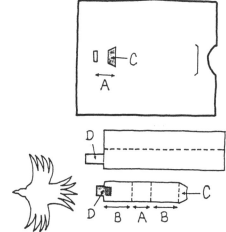

This example is built onto flap Mechanism **94**.
Length A on the base equals A on the parallelogram, lengths B are the same.
Stick tab C to the base and tab D to the pull-strip. In this design the card at D is double thickness and doesn't need further strengthening. The parallelogram can be added to either side of the flap.

100.

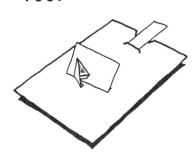 

 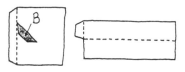

This example is built onto flap Mechanism **95**.
Having made the flap, other pop-up pieces can be added to the gully formed between the flap and the base. In this example a simple V-Fold. A sticks to A on the base, B to B on the flap.
Arms can be added to this, see Mechanism **73**.

101. DELAYED DOUBLE-ACTION FLAPS

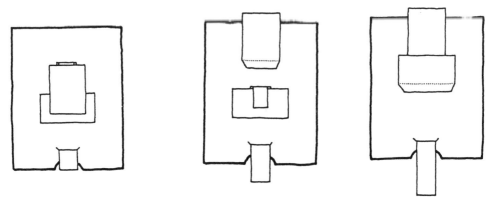

As the strip is pulled, first one flap lifts then, after a delay, so does the other. These flaps are based on Mechanism **94**.

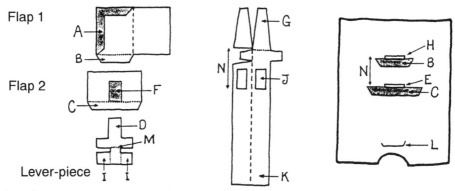

Construction:

Flap 1 is a pocket, fold it over and stick along the two edges A.

Stick flap 1 to the base, B to B. Stick flap 2 to the base, C to C.

Push D on the lever-piece up through slot E. Stick D to F on flap 2.

The end of the pull-strip G is tapered. Push the end G up through slot H and into the pocket of flap 1. Do not put glue on this.

Fold the two tabs I on the lever-piece, push them down through window J in the pull-strip and then unfold them again.

Thread the end of the pull-strip K through slit L in the base.

Fold crease M so that the end of the lever-piece which has passed through the window J lies flat.

Length N on the pull-strip equals N on the base.

Add a backing sheet, glued round the edges of the base.

How it works:

The pocket construction of Flap 1 allows the pull-strip to lift it and then continue sliding. The window J allows the strip to slide a little way before it engages with the lever-piece and lifts flap 2.

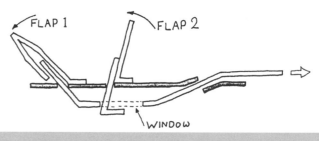

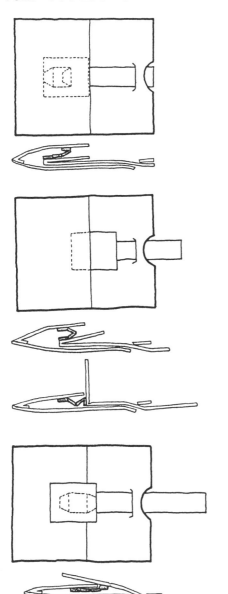

The flap is the end of the pull-strip. When the strip is pushed in, the flap lies folded over under the mask. The back of the flap is attached to the underside of the mask by the multi-creased strip. As the Pull-strip is pulled and the flap slides out from under the mask, the multi-creased strip comes into action and flips the flap over.
Precise measuring is essential.

The multi-creased strip has three creases, these are parallel and 1cm. apart. It has a tab on each end, A and D, these are 1 cm wide

Tab A sticks to B on the back of the masking piece. Length C is 2 cm.
Tab D sticks to E on the back of the flap. It is important that crease F is not adjacent to the valley fold G, it is 1cm. away.

Length H equals length C. In this case they are both 2cm.
The length of flap J is C + H + one tab, in this case J = 5 cm.

Push end K through slit L, then stick the masking piece down round the edges of the base.

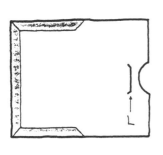

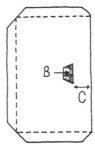

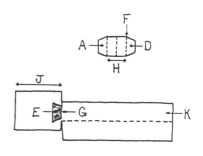

103. THE HUB

This mechanism holds pieces of card together while allowing them to rotate. It is very useful when combined with pull-strips.

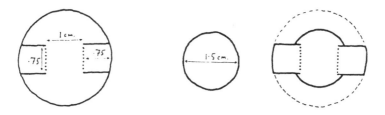

A disc is scored and cut to form two arms which can fold upwards. The arms fold up and pass through a hole in a piece of card. The arms are folded out flat again on top of the piece of card. Another small disc can be stuck onto the arms to hold it all in place. Follow the dimensions in the diagram. If the hole is too big the mechanism will tend to drift, and if the hole is too small it grips the hub and can't turn.

104. ROTATING WINDOW

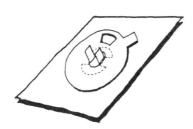
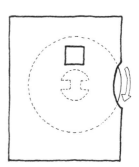

A large disc with a window in it rotates on the page. The images are on the base behind the disc. As the disc turns, different images come into view. Alternatively, the window can be cut in the base. The images are on the disc which rotates behind the base.

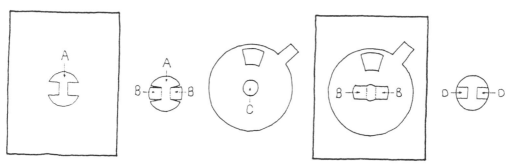

On the hub, spread glue on the underside of part A, then stick it to the base. Fold up the tabs B, push them through hole C, then fold them out flat again. Put small dabs of glue on top of B and B, then stick the small disc D on top. This strengthens the whole construction.

105. THE SLIDING PIVOT

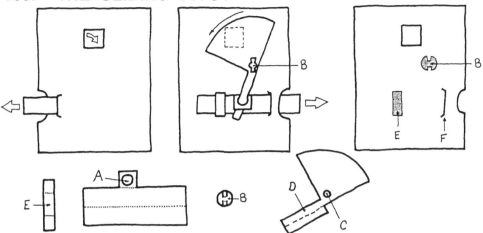

This mechanism uses a hub, a pull-strip (see Mechanism **84**) and a sliding-pivot to produce movement behind a window in the base.

The pull-strip has a flap projecting from one side. The flap has a circular hole in it A. The moving image-piece is held to the back of the base by a hub B. The hub's arms go through hole C in the image-piece. The image-piece has an arm projecting from it D, this goes through hole A. The width of the arm should be slightly less than the diameter of the hole. Add a backing sheet to strengthen and protect the mechanism.

The nearer the pull-strip lies to the hub, the more the mechanism moves. The movement is controlled by the flap coming up against sleeve E and slit F.

106. THE PULL-BAR

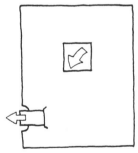

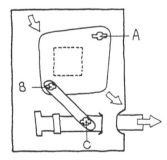

This mechanism produces movement in a different direction to the one at the top of the page. Hub A attaches the moving image-piece to the back of the base. The pull-bar is linked to the image-piece by hub B, and the pull-strip by C.

107. RETRACTING STRIP

Hub A holds the pull-bar to the pull-strip.
Hub B holds the pull-bar to the image-piece.
The image passes through slit C to the front
of the page. In this case making the slit C only
very slightly wider than the image-piece
controls the direction in which the image moves.

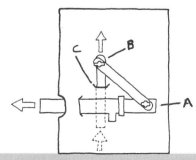

108.   THE FIXED PIVOT

 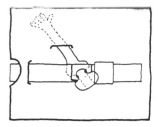

An arm waves as the pull-strip strip is pulled. The arm moves in the opposite direction to the pull-strip.

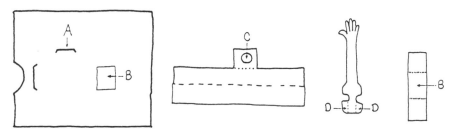

Slit A is the simplest type of pivot, the moving arm passes through it.
The nearer the pull-strip is to slit A, the more the arm on the front moves.

The length of slit A compared to the width of the arm is important:
If the slit is too long the arm will drift.
If the slit is too short the arm's diagonal movement is restricted.

Sleeve B holds the pull-strip to the base. The pull-strip has a flap on one side with a circular hole in it C. The end of the arm has two tabs D which attach it to the pull-strip. These tabs are folded to pass through the hole C, and then unfolded.

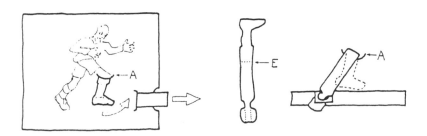

The image can be made to move in the same direction as the pull strip:
Score and fold line E on the moving image-piece, crease the fold firmly. This fold stays behind the base. Make sure that fold E is not too close to slit A or they may tangle and jam. Add a backing sheet, glued on around the edges of the base. This holds all the pieces flat and helps them to move smoothly.

109. MULTIPLE MOVING ARMS

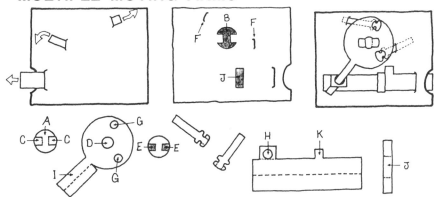

The hub A sticks to the back of the base at B. Its arms C go through the central hole D in the large rotating disc. The arms fold flat again and the small disc is stuck onto them to strengthen the hub, E sticks to C.

The moving-image arms go through slits F in the base, they are attached to the large rotating disc using holes G, see Mechanism **108** opposite.

The pull-strip has a flap with a circular hole in it H, the arm on the rotating disc I goes through the hole. J is a sleeve which holds the pull-strip to the back of the base. K is a tab on the pull-strip which prevents the pull-strip from pushing in too far.

With its four different types of pivot this mechanism is well worth experimenting with.

110. ROCKING MOTION

Moving the pull-strip makes the image rock.

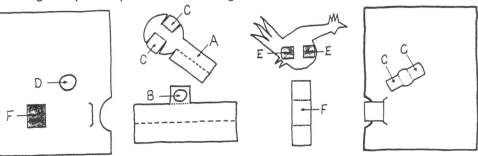

The arm A on the hub goes through hole B in the flap on the pull-strip. The hub's tabs C go through hole D in the base, then fold out flat. The rocking image sticks onto them, E sticks to C. Sleeve F holds and guides the pull-strip.

111. ARTICULATED IMAGES

Two hubs, A and B, link three image-pieces into a chain. The two ends of the chain are attached to the base by two more hubs. The tabs on hub C pass through hole D in the base. The movement is generated by hub E, based on Mechanism **110**. Its tabs go through hole F and then have the other end of the chain stuck onto them. The arm G on hub E goes through the hole in the flap on the   pull-strip

Several chains can be attached to the main moving image.
Hub A links through the base to the pull strip. Hubs B and C hold the ends of the arms to the base. The other four hubs link up the moving parts of the image.

112.   ARTICULATED POP-UP IMAGE

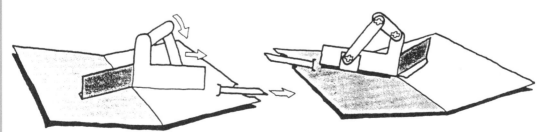

Hubs can be combined with V-Folds to produce articulated pop-up images. To see how to adapt the pull-strip refer to Mechanism **91**.

113. SWOOP MOVEMENT

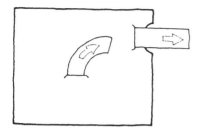 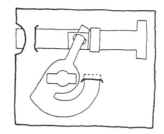

As the strip is pulled an image curves into view across the base.

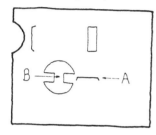 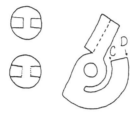 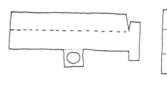

The disc and extending image are cut from one piece of card.
The construction of the hub, pull-strip and large rotating disc is all the same as in Mechanism **105.**

When making this mechanism make sure that the slit in the base A is aligned with the centre of the hub B. On the extending image-piece, the edges C and D are concentric arcs also centred on point B.

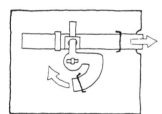 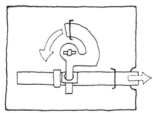 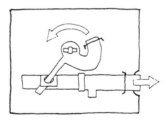

The image can be made to extend in different directions by adjusting the relative positions of the pull-strip, hub, arm and extending image.

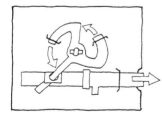 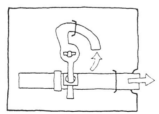 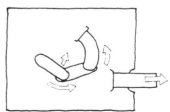

More than one image can extend. The image can be made to withdraw instead of extending. Articulation can be added to the end of the image, see opposite page.

A backing sheet is needed on these mechanisms. The movement generates twist at the weak points of the main hub-piece. The backing sheet holds everything flush against the page.

114. SPIRALS

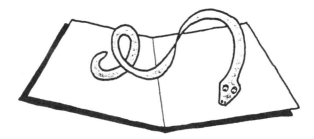

This is a very simple and effective mechanism. The key to making it is in the sticking method.

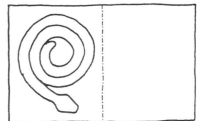

Before gluing, place the spiral on the left hand page and check that it doesn't jut out over the spine or edge of the page.

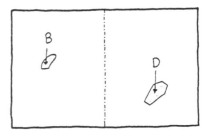

Spread glue on the underside of of the tail end A. Stick it in the desired position on the base, B. Then spread glue on the top side of the head end, C. Close the base and press firmly, C will find its natural sticking position, D.

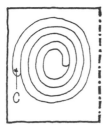

Adjusting the position of end C in relation to the spine affects the shape of the popped-up spiral.

More than one spiral can be used simultaneously on the same base. The sticking is a little tricky, but the effect is magnificently chaotic.

The spiral does not have to be circular, other shapes work well. Make sure they are long enough as well as narrow.

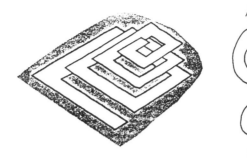

Unexpected effects make this mechanism worth experimenting with.

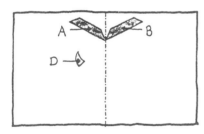

Small pieces can be stuck on to the spiral after it is stuck to the base.

Spirals can be added to many other mechanisms. In this case one is built onto a V-Fold. Remember to always use the gluing method explained opposite, in which the second sticking position is found by closing the base.

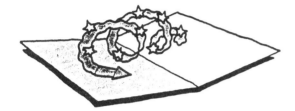

First stick the V-Fold to the base, A and B. Then stick the underside of C to D. Now almost close the base, check how the V-Fold comes down on the spiral and work out the exact position for putting the spot of glue, E. Finally close the base so that the end sticks in its natural position F.

115.

Short twists can pop-up. Make a crease and a tab at each end of the pop-up piece. Then use the gluing method explained opposite to attach it to the base.

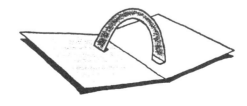

116. AUTOMATIC STRIP

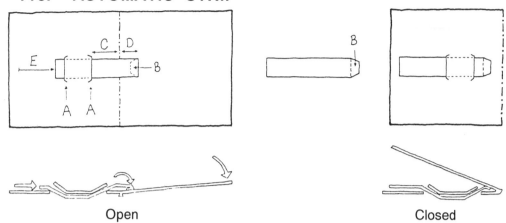

Open   Closed

As the base opens it pulls a strip. The automatic pull-strip can be used to raise a flap or pop-up mechanism in the middle of one of the pages.

Thread the strip through both slits A, then stick tab B on the strip to B on the base. The length C must be greater than length D. The movement generated at E is exactly double length D.

AUTOMATIC FLAP

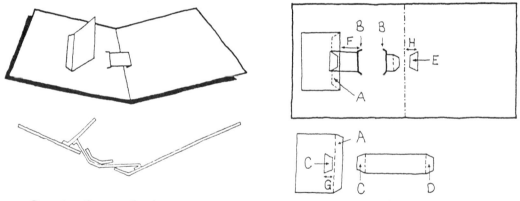

Construction method:
Stick A on the flap to A on the base. Thread the strip through the two slits B. Stick C on the strip to C on the flap. Put glue on tab D, then close the base and press firmly, tab D finds its correct sticking place E.

Measurements: F must be greater than G. G can't be less than H.
To flip flap right over G = H. To lift flap at an angle, G is greater than H.

These lengths can be adjusted so that when the base is open the flap stands vertically on the base, then parallelogram Mechanisms (see **99**) can be built onto the flap.

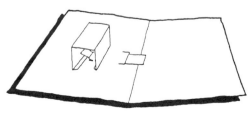

117. BOWING SHAPE

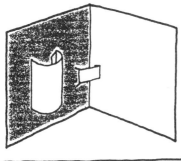

The automatic strip can be used to pull up a curved surface.

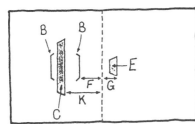

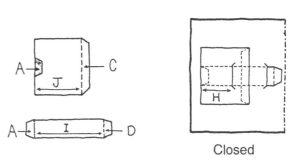

Closed

To construct this mechanism:

Stick tab A on the strip to A on the underside of the bowing piece. Thread the strip through the two slits B. Stick tab C on the bowing piece to C on the base. Spread glue on tab D, then close the base. Tab D will stick to E.

Getting the lengths right is very important:

Length F must be greater than G. H is more than 2 x G. I equals J + K - G.

To hide the section of strip which is visible above the spine construct a parallelogram or a quadrilateral above it, see Mechanisms **34** and **54.**

AUTOMATIC PULL-STRIP ABOVE THE PAGE

In this variation the pull-strip does not pass through slits in the base.

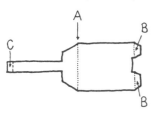

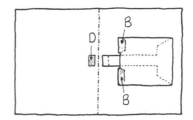

Fold over along crease A. Position the piece so that the pull-strip is underneath and protrudes between tabs B. Tab C should lie about 1cm from the spine. Stick the tabs B to the page. Finally put glue on tab C, then close the page and press firmly so that tab C finds its natural sticking position D.

118. STAGE SET

The mechanism has a series of receding planes that create a stage set effect when the base is open. All the pieces have a central valley fold that folds away backwards as the base is closed.

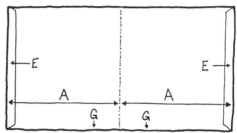

Lengths A are longer than B, and lengths B are longer than C. Tabs D stick to the front of E, and tabs F stick to the back of E.

The plane nearest the viewer is the narrowest. Its width determines how far the base can open. Stick this piece on last.

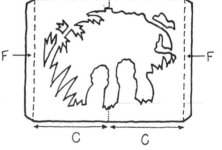

By putting glueing tabs on the bottom of line G the whole mechanism can be mounted on another base and turned into a V-Fold, see Mechanism **1**.

119. SHUTTER SCENE

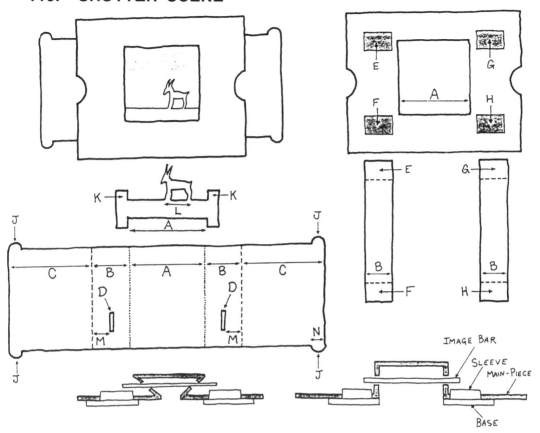

When the large tabs at the side of the base are pulled the shutters slide open to reveal a multi layered scene.

The main-piece of the mechanism is a long, broad, strip; it has five sections. The middle section A is the back of the revealed scene. The two sections B are the side walls of the scene; these have slots in them D that the image-bar is suspended from. The sections C are the shutters, their outer edges are the tabs that are pulled to open the scene. When they are pushed in they meet in the middle.

The two sleeves are stuck to the back of the base on each side of the window, E, F, G, H. They hold the main-piece in place and stop sections C from sliding out too far. Note the extensions J that stop the shutters pushing in too far.

The image-bar has tabs on the end, K, that stop it slipping out of slots D. The positioning of the slots in sections B is important. As the mechanism closes, the slots move closer together, sliding along the image-bar. The width of the image L must be less than the distance between the slots when the scene is in the closed position. L is less than 2 x M. Several image-bars can be used.

Lengths are important:
A is the same on the main-piece and on the base. B is half of A. The sleeve width is also B. C equals A + N. The total width of the base is 2 x C.

120. SAWING NOISE

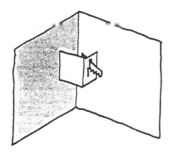 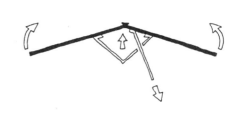

This mechanism makes a rattling noise as the base is opened. The key is a serrated strip that passes through a specially shaped slot cut in one plane of a quadrilateral! (See Mechanism **55**). As the base opens and closes the serrated blade is pushed and pulled through the slot.

The top part of the slot, above cut A, is 2 mm wide and is removed. This part guides the saw blade. The bottom part of the slot, below cut A, is a flap that rattles against the saw's teeth.

Use a double thickness of card to make the saw. The gluing-tab, at the base of the saw, is at 90° to the saw blade. The tab sticks to the base parallel to the spine.

Line A on the slot must lie precisely between the top and bottom of the saw's teeth.

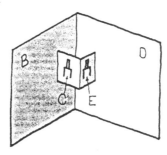

The side of the base that the saw sticks on to, and the plane in which the slot is cut must be on adjacent sides; if the saw is attached to base B it must project through slot C. A saw attached to base D goes through slot E.